THE LOST GIRL

A Neverland Story

Allison Spooner

CHAPTER 1

The moment Angela's feet pressed into the soggy earth of her destination, she wanted to turn around and go home. The moment the damp air touched her face and the sound of waves crashing against cliffs reached her ears, Angela knew her mother's bizarre plan had worked, and she immediately wished it hadn't. When a cool breeze tickled her hair, bringing with it the smell of fresh grass, moist air, and dirt and salt water rather than the smell of her mom's lavender perfume, she wanted to cry, not rejoice. When cold air wrapped around her and all she had to pull tighter was her thick, gray sweater instead of her favorite weighted blanket, she wanted to keep her eyes shut until she was back in her window seat, in her room, holding her mom's hand. She wanted to open her tightly shut eyes and see her mom smiling back at her, reassuring her that it was OK if she didn't want to do this, that she could stay home and they would figure something out like they always did. But she knew what she would see instead. She'd heard the stories too many times.

When Angela finally did open her eyes, it was not to the bright blue skies, lush green forests, or emerald and teal seas she'd grown up hearing about. No. It was to a thick, heavy fog that obscured her view of almost everything around her. This wasn't the Neverland she knew. If it was possible to truly know a place you'd never been, Angela felt as though she knew Neverland through her mother's stories and books—and this was not the place she'd described. Maybe she was on the wrong fantastical island. Maybe this wasn't where Lost Boys and pirates lived together under multiple shining suns, the days burning hot until they faded away into temperate nights. Maybe she'd gone to the *third* star to the right instead of the second . . .

She looked up. Where were the suns? She shivered and pulled the oversized, cable-knit sweater closer. Where was the warmth those two suns should provide? She could see a yellow glow behind the thick wall of fog, but nothing else. Angela shifted from one soggy foot to another and turned in a small circle in the spot where she stood. What was she supposed to do now?

Then she heard her mother's voice, whispering the advice she always gave when Angela was stressed or unsure. *"Take a breath, darling. Calm your mind, calm your heart, and the answer will come."* So Angela closed her eyes and took a deep breath through her nose, the moisture in the air coating her lungs, and then let it out through her mouth. She repeated the flow, but on the second exhale, a crack to her right made her jump. Her eyes snapped open as she turned toward the sound.

"Who's there?" She'd meant to shout it, but it came out as more of a strangled whisper. She cleared her throat. As she squinted into the fog, looking for the source of the sound, she didn't have to squint as hard. She took another deep breath, and the air tickling her nose was just a little warmer. She reached out in front of her and could see just a little farther. She let out her breath and the last of the fog rolled down the hills she could now see surrounding her. She pulled another breath in and looked up. There were the suns. She gave a small smile as their warmth finally reached her cheeks. Letting her breath out, she almost giggled as a warm breeze pushed the rest of the fog away and tickled the hair around her ears.

"Oh, there you are, Neverland," she whispered as she took a step forward and let her eyes dance over a horizon of green waves and sparkling blue pools. This looked right. This was—

"Who are you talking to?"

Angela gasped and whirled around, the spell broken.

If she'd had any doubt about where she was, the scene before her confirmed she was in the right place. Standing there in a disorderly line was a wall of adolescent, disheveled boys with wild hair and narrowed eyes, each one brandishing a sword, knife, or makeshift weapon. They were all dressed in various combinations of what looked like leather or faded and ripped cloth and greenery. And they were all filthy. She took a step back and almost tripped. They all jumped at her sudden movement but did not retreat.

"I . . ." Angela motioned weakly around her in a feeble attempt to answer their shouted question, but they didn't wait for more of an answer.

The one standing nearest to her spoke, inching his weapon closer to her with each word. "Who are you? Is he with you?"

Of course, she knew immediately who he meant.

"Oh, no . . ." Her voice shook as she took a step back, eyeing the blade he was holding. She'd been looking around them, trying to get a glimpse at the world that was finally revealing itself, but when she realized what she had to tell them, these crazy-eyed children pointing weapons at her, she stopped searching and looked directly at the one who had spoken.

He had bright red hair and a spattering of freckles across his nose and he lifted an eyebrow as he waited for an answer.

"I–I'm sorry but he . . . he died." She tensed, waiting for their response, but they were looking beyond her. They were looking for *him*, sure he would drop from the sky with a devilish grin, laughing at the great joke he'd played on them.

But there was no one else. Just her, a thirteen-year-old girl, looking for the fastest way to get back home.

"Died? But how? Fighting pirates in the other world?"

"On a great adventure?"

The circle they had formed around her got tighter with each question. These boys had been friends with Peter, but she also knew what they were capable of when faced with a threat. And at that moment, *she* was a threat. She glanced behind her, searching for a quick escape.

"N-no. He . . . he died in his bed. He was very old. Do you know how I get ho—?" But her question was drowned out.

There was a spatter of chattering at the word "old," like a group of squirrels who just watched the tree with their winter nut storage go up in flames.

She heard whispers of, "But he promised . . ." and "Again?" before the red-haired boy turned back to her.

"You lie. Neverland told us he was coming."

She sucked in her breath at the word "Neverland." It was true then, she was here. Her mom was right. She hated it when her mom was right.

The redhead swiped his sword toward the landscape behind him, and the boy closest to him ducked to avoid the carelessly flung blade. She followed the motion and noticed that the last of the fog had truly faded and that the dark and gloomy sky behind him, now visible through the receding haze, was changing before her eyes. A bright blue center was chasing off gray edges, and on the horizon, a rainbow was forming over the outline of a distant mountain range. The trees were now swaying in the wind, almost vibrating with energy and life.

"The suns are shining again and the trees are dancing," the boy said. "Neverland has been a still and quiet place for a very long time. Today, it woke up."

The boy backed up and lifted his chin, studying her from head to toe with sparkling green eyes. His gaze narrowed. "I'll ask again. Who are you? Why have you come?"

Trying her best to ignore his blade, Angela puffed out her chest and placed her hands on her hips. Her mom's stories were true. Neverland existed. Peter Pan was real, and she was his descendant. "I am Angela Margaret Johnson, great-granddaughter of your Pan." If she was going to embrace her heritage, this was the place to do it.

But the line didn't land like she expected.

"How do we know?" shouted a voice from the circle.

"What if she's a pirate?"

"Isn't she a *lady*?"

"Ladies can't be pirates!"

"How did she get here?"

Clearly unimpressed, the boy arched an eyebrow and stepped closer so that his freckled face was barely inches from hers. Before she could stop him, he leaned over and, his red hair tickling her cheek, sucked in her scent. He stepped back and turned toward the boys. "She smells like Peter. Neverland is awake. She could be telling the truth."

Angela flinched and sniffed at her shoulder, trying to figure out what Peter Pan might smell like.

"We need more proof!" a voice shouted.

The boy turned back to Angela. "We need more proof."

She lifted her empty hands slightly and glanced down. How was she supposed to prove her heritage? The fairy dust from her mom had worn off and she could no longer fly. She wasn't carrying any pictures, and she looked more like her mother than her grandfather.

Searching her mind for any fact that might prove her identity, she realized she had a wealth of information instantly available. She'd grown up with a woman who wrote about Peter Pan for a living. Peter's granddaughter had spent her childhood listening to him tell tales of Neverland, the tales that no one else knew, and she'd spent the rest of her life writing them down and putting them out into the world.

"It's kind of a long story." One she wasn't really sure she wanted to get into at the moment. She was feeling a little overwhelmed as it dawned on her that if her mom's plan had worked, that meant she was a million stars away, not by her side as she had been Angela's entire life. She swallowed and looked at the ground, wondering how disappointed her mother would be if Angela just turned around and came home. As she looked up, she saw dozens of pairs of legs fold and tuck under butts as all the Lost Boys sat cross-legged on the ground in front of her. "I'd really rather just go—"

"Tell us your story."

She sighed, pulling her sweater tighter around her. Maybe if she told them how she got there, they could tell her how to get home. She thought back to the moments that had brought her to Neverland. She started with Peter's story as her mother had told it, and then her own sad tale.

***

"Peter Pan wasn't killed by a pirate's sword. He didn't die in battle or at the hands of an enemy. He died on his own terms, in his own time.

"It was his choice," she insisted as concern clouded the faces of her audience. "Peter Pan outran his fate for many years, and when all his adventures had been had and all his games had been played, he knew it was time to face his final adventure. And when the last breath finally left his body, his skin still smelled like a cool breeze on a hot summer day." Every head in her little audience nodded, and she wondered if that's what the boy had smelled on her.

"He died surrounded by the family he'd created when he left Neverland. A son, a daughter, an array of grandchildren of all ages, and my mother, Moira, the smallest of the group."

By the time fate finally caught up with him, his own children had gone swiftly about the business of growing up. He couldn't blame them really, given that he'd once chosen to do that very same thing. After their abduction and their rescue by the father who rediscovered his past and his memories, Pan's two kids tried to share their stories. But by that time the world was already a much less friendly place for the imagination of a child. When they'd tried to tell the world about their adventures in Neverland, that they'd been kidnapped by the notorious Captain James Hook and their dad, the great Peter Pan, had recaptured his youth and come to their rescue, they were ridiculed for their tales, laughed out of their faith, and inevitably convinced their adventures never happened. It broke his heart when they stopped believing. He knew what that felt like and he didn't want that for his children. But whenever he brought up their adventures, they rolled their eyes and insisted he must have been dreaming. They passed their practicality on to their children, and they all shook their heads and smiled when Grandpa Peter talked about Neverland. All except one.

The great Peter Pan passed the last years of his life in his bed, sharing his adventures with little Mo, the daughter of his daughter, willing her to remember, to share his story, to believe. And she did.

"Mo grew up too. But she took Peter and Neverland, and"—Angela nodded toward her audience—"the Lost Boys with her. She'd promised her grandpa she would tell the world the rest of his story, tell them about the years after he left, and when he returned, and all the games and adventures he shared with his Lost Boys after Hook was defeated and he found his memories again. Because those were happy times, he'd told her, the years he got back. They were a gift.

"And my mom shared that gift with the world. She made it her job and she's really good at it."

The boys shifted and some smiled. They seemed to like this, the idea that it was someone's job to share Peter's stories.

And then it was time for *her* story.

She told them about her cancer diagnosis. She skipped over all the years of treatments and despair and bad news and instead told them about the moments that had brought her to Neverland.

"How am I even getting there?" she'd asked skeptically from her window seat as her mom dug around in a trunk that had once belonged to her grandfather. The keepsake Moira's family had kept hidden and locked up through most of her mother's childhood. The trunk Moira asked after and begged to take with her when she'd moved out. The trunk Moira came into possession of only after a long battle with her family, who had wanted to sell it to a Pan museum. Angela knew her mom would eventually donate it to the museum, but there'd been something in it Moira needed first. After a moment, her mom emerged from the chest with a grin, holding a small cloth bag as though it contained all their answers.

"What if I don't want to go?" Angela asked, eyeing the bag suspiciously.

"You have to," her mom said. "There are no other options. This is your life we're talking about here. Modern medicine has failed us, we're on our own. And what do we do when we're on our own?"

Angela considered not giving the usual response. She thought about staying silent or breaking down and crying and telling her that, honestly, she kind of wanted to give up. But one look at her mom's face and she knew that wasn't even an option. "We fight," said Angela with as much strength as her failing body could muster.

Moira smiled. "I just need you to be OK, my darling."

Of course, Moira had been right. After the doctor had given his firm and final diagnosis, they'd really had no other options.

No more chemo, no more radiation, no more surgery, no more throwing up or hair loss or shivering while sweating and holding on to her mom's arm through waves of nausea. They'd tried everything possible to fight the cancer now spreading through her blood unchecked and unrestrained. Now it was time to try the impossible. And if it made her mom happy, Angela was willing to try anything.

But her mom didn't seem to think it was so impossible, finding this world where children could live and play forever. Now that she had the trunk and that little bag, the world where trees were houses and grassy hills were beds and fairies were playmates and pirates were the only threat, was within reach. Moira had believed in Neverland since she was a little girl, and she was gambling everything on that belief.

"Just think happy thoughts," Moira had whispered as she shook the cloth bag, sprinkling its treasured contents over her daughter's head, "and don't forget to give the boys Grandpa Peter's message."

Happy thoughts after the years they'd just been through? But, as skeptical as Angela was, she could have sworn she felt a tickle on the back of her ears, and with her mom's words, she couldn't help remembering the days before cancer, when her body was strong enough to do yoga with her mom every morning before school, when they would wander flea markets for hours, using her mom's royalty checks to fill their home with unique items reminiscent of the days when Peter Pan was first written about.

The next time she opened her eyes, she was surrounded by an inky-black sky, chasing twinkling lights that could have been stars and could have been fairies and she heard her mom's voice echoing, *"Second star to the right and straight on till morning . . ."*

She'd closed her eyes against the chill of the cool night air and let the black wrap around her like a blanket, trying to outrun her fate and soak in the moment all at the same time. Like Peter Pan before her, she was trying to manipulate the inevitable.

She tried to ignore the fact that even Peter Pan, the eternal child, had chosen to accept time instead of running from it, embrace life instead of holding it still, and finally pay the same price that all humans eventually pay. But he'd chosen that fate. He'd chosen to come back from Neverland, start a family, and give up eternity. If he chose that, couldn't she choose the opposite? Couldn't she choose to fight the word "terminal" with the word "eternal" and embrace all that his boyhood home had to offer?

***

"And then, I was just here." She shrugged. "It was like I'd known where to find it all along."

The boys nodded knowingly at this, maybe the only thing she'd said so far they could truly relate to.

As her voice trailed off, they all continued to stare, and with at least ten pre-teen boys gazing up at her, she began to feel a little self-conscious. Tugging at her sweater, her hand went to her short, brown hair. She still forgot that most of it was gone except for a pile of curls on top of her head, the curls that had come back after chemo. And then, someone spoke up.

"What's cancer?"

"Oh, umm . . . It's a sickness."

"A sickness?"

"Yea . . . Like, the flu?"

Blank stares.

"A cold?"

More confusion. Then they changed course.

"Why did Peter stop coming?"

"Why didn't he say goodbye?"

"Oh." She thought back to her mom's request and the words she'd made her memorize. "He said he never meant for his last trip here to be his last trip. He just got tired and, well, old."

"Like Wendy?"

"Yes, like Wendy."

She continued. "He's sorry that he stopped coming, but he wants you all to know he never forgot you, not once. You were his Lost Boys until the end."

She waited for some sort of reaction, maybe some emotion, but the boys continued to stare and the silence dragged on. She bounced from one foot to the other, silently hoping the movement would send her airborne and she could fly away.

Finally, the red–haired boy said, "OK."

Well, she thought, that was . . . anticlimactic.

And then, more questions.

"So, *why* are you here?" the same boy asked.

She sighed. She was getting a little annoyed with the third degree. Yes, this was their home, but it was her heritage.

"I . . . I'm sick and I don't want to be."

He cocked his head to one side. He still didn't understand.

Neverland did not understand sickness. People didn't just die in Neverland; they were killed by a pirate's sword or doing daring deeds, never by illness or old age. Well, that was good news for her.

She tried again. "I'm here because I'm a Pan and I deserve to be."

"She knows Pan's story," a voice from the back squeaked. "I believe her!"

The red-haired boy whipped around to face the voice. "We can see she is who she says she is. She woke up Neverland, she smells like Peter. Her stories are true. But we still don't know *why* she is here!"

She sighed, knowing exactly what she needed to say. "I'm here to always be a little girl and to have fun."

This was the answer they were waiting for. The boy nodded seriously, and the rest of them jumped up from their spots in the grass, grinning.

"Then fun you shall have. Welcome to Neverland, Lady Pan. Let's play."

CHAPTER 2

At the word "play," the other boys cheered and took off, marching down the hill on which she'd landed, leaving her running to catch up. No one told her their names, no one told her where they were going—they just went. She supposed that was the norm here in Neverland.

"Hey! Wait up!" she called, struggling to match their energy, mostly because she didn't want to be left alone in a strange land and she still hadn't figured out how to get home.

As they marched through the tall grasses, sloping hills, and damp marshes of a bright and pleasant Neverland (very different from the one she'd landed in), the boy who had deemed her Lady Pan was pointing out landmarks. "See, Lady Pan? Down that hill is another hideout, and just beyond that is the tree where Peter made Wendy's house," he said, pointing his sword to his right.

"*Angela*," she tried for the third or fifth time. "My name isn't actually Pan."

The boy only stared.

"Okay," she sighed. "Lady Pan is fine. What's your name?"

She was less interested in the landscape than she was in learning about these boys. If they wouldn't tell her how to get home, there was a good chance they'd be spending an awful lot of time together in the near future.

He puffed out his chest. "They call me Jax."

"And you're the leader?"

He shrugged. "Pan is our leader."

"But Pan has been gone a long time."

"Fine, then I am the leader until Pan returns."

Oh great, she thought. Apparently, "he died" wasn't a clear enough indication that their leader would *not* be returning. She changed the subject. "Where exactly are we going, Jax?"

"To get our lagoon back from the pirates."

She stopped walking. "Wait . . . what?!"

He turned from a few paces ahead of her. "The pirates took the lagoon when Pan left and Neverland darkened. Without Pan, we've mostly stayed hidden or on the other side of the island. But now, a Pan has returned."

Angela's mouth fell open, closed, and then opened again. There was so much to say, but this boy, this Jax with his wild red hair, freckles, and a sword almost longer than he was tall, had briefly stolen her words.

When she didn't respond, he cocked his head. "You don't *want* to fight the pirates?"

"No . . . I mean, well . . . you know I'm not Pan, right?" She didn't think this very important fact was sinking in.

He tilted his head in the other direction. "But that *is* your name. Lady Pan."

She grabbed at the strands of the short curls on top of her head in frustration. She used to tug the ends of her shoulder-length hair when she was mad, but chemo took that small luxury away from her.

"But . . . I'm not . . . I'm just *related* to him. I never even met him! He's my family. Don't you have a family?"

His head bowed for a moment. "I think I did, once." And then he started walking again.

The rest of the boys had not stopped to wait for them, and he jogged to catch up. She watched after him for a second in wonder. These boys didn't understand sickness or the possibility of death, or even family, but she was beginning to think they did understand her need to find solace in the wild and welcoming Neverland. She grew up knowing that most Lost Boys were the boys who fell out of their prams when they were babies, but as she grew, she realized that most of the inhabitants of Neverland were probably running from something, like Pan . . . like her.

Angela ran behind him, shouting. "So you think that on

my first day in Neverland, I want to fight pirates just because I'm part of Pan's family?"

"Of course," he yelled over his shoulder.

"Of course," she whispered under her breath, panting.

***

They reached the base of another large hill, and the whole group stopped and turned to face her. She was trying very hard to look as though she wasn't winded, but she hadn't had this much activity in a long time, and the idea of scaling the hill in front of them was making her weak in the knees.

"The lagoon is just on the other side," Jax said.

"Okay . . . ," she said putting her hands on her hips, trying to steady her breath. She could tell by the expectant gaze of ten or more sets of eyes that she was supposed to have a better response. It occurred to her that they thought she was leading this crazy expedition.

"What's the plan?" Jax asked, confirming her suspicion.

"Plan!?" She had no intention of leading an attack on the pirates this early on in her adventures—it just didn't seem wise. "Why am I in charge?"

"You're a Pan! Pan was always in charge."

"OK, then. How about we turn around, go to one of the dozens of hideouts you showed me, and you all can tell me how I get *home*?"

The Lost Boys stared.

"I thought we were going to fight the pirates," came a voice from the group.

The other boys cheered at the suggestion.

Angela shifted. This was a little like being the only one in the class who wanted to continue silent reading time instead of going out to play in a foot of snow at recess. "I've never even *seen* a pirate before!"

"What? Are you *scared?*" Jax taunted.

She shot him a scathing look before she could stop herself. She hadn't come to Neverland to be made fun of, but she also wasn't afraid to admit her feelings.

"Yes!" she answered and Jax's head jerked back.

This response caught him off guard, and his mouth opened and closed a few times before he shot, "You're *nothing* like Peter!"

The boys gave an "Ohhhh," at the insult, and Angela rolled her eyes.

"Because I'm NOT Peter. I'm far away from my home and my mom, and I'm surrounded by strangers who want me to fight *pirates*, for crying out loud. So, yes. I'm scared!"

The boys were quiet for a moment while they waited to see who would respond next. Then a small voice rose from the center of the group.

"You're right," it said, and Angela strained her neck to see where it was coming from. A boy smaller than the rest, so small he was calling out from atop another boy's shoulders so he could see through the group, crawled down from his perch and approached her. He was about a foot shorter than her and most of his Lost Boy companions. His limbs were long and wiry. He had a tuft of pale blond hair that stood up at the back and his lips were thin and pointed. His blue eyes were full of concern. Once he was in front of her, he nodded.

"The pirates are scary."

"Aw, c'mon, Pidge. We used to fight the pirates all the time!" Jax rolled his eyes at the smaller boy, and Angela immediately felt for him.

"Well, I don't really like it!" He turned back to Angela. "But if I can do it, you can do it!" He jumped as he spoke his last words, his voice squeaking.

Angela smirked and looked at Jax, who scoffed. She knew she wasn't going to get anywhere with the "I've never even fought a pirate" argument, so she changed course. "OK, Jax. We'll keep going, but I think you know the pirates and the landscape better than I do, so I am hereby granting you permission to take the lead on this mission."

Jax looked to the other boys, his eyebrows furrowed. He leaned over and whispered to the closest boy, "Pan would never do something like that!"

"Pan only cared about being in charge," she said, using her knowledge of her great-grandfather's younger days with the Lost Boys. "A true leader uses the strengths of their team to their advantage. Our strength is your knowledge of the land and the enemy . . . and I am using it."

He still didn't seem to understand why a leader would hand over power so easily, but he glanced once more at the Lost Boys, and when they offered no advice, he relented. "OK," he said, aiming his sword at the top of the hill. "We will observe from the top and make a plan from there. Now, we climb."

"I was afraid you'd say that," she mumbled.

At the top of the hill, she gasped, and not just because she could hardly breathe. She now understood why the lagoon was such a coveted spot. The waters were a bright blue under the shining suns, and the vast waves from the ocean surrounding it were blocked by the circle of land protecting the sparkling pool. A channel led from the ocean to fill the cove, but other than that, it was completely protected. The hill they now stood on provided a grassy backdrop, and she knew, not because she could see it, but because of what she'd read and had been told to her, that there was a cave carved into the rock of the cliffside below them.

It was a beautiful and peaceful spot, and anyone playing or resting in it would be completely hidden and protected from the outside world. But it appeared that the outside world had made its way in. In the center of the calm, sparkling waters, sporting a black-and-white skull-and-crossbones flag waving in the now gentle breeze, sat the giant and sprawling *Jolly Roger*, the ship that haunted the dreams of so many children. It was amazing that the ship could even fit inside the cozy cove, and it was a jarring sight to see such a menacing structure in such a peaceful setting.

But, of course, only hours ago the mood of the lagoon had matched the appearance of the ship. Like Jax had said, the moment she landed, Neverland woke up.

"It's so beautiful," she whispered.

"Yea . . . now," said Jax, coming up beside her. "Neverland doesn't like it when Pan is gone. It's happier when he's here."

Angela thought back on the fog and gloom that had surrounded her when she'd landed in Neverland and realized that it must have been like that all the time before she'd arrived. Apparently, Peter Pan's DNA was all Neverland needed to be happy again. The Lost Boys were excited and energized by this change in the wind, but it appeared the pirates were not.

"What's happening?" she asked as they watched the movement of the pirates from the top of the hill.

At the bow of the ship danced a short, round man with wild gray hair reaching out from the sides of his head and a shiny patch on top reflecting the vibrant sunlight. He was practically jumping up and down while he shouted orders and questions to men who, it seemed, were only kind of paying attention. He reminded her of a substitute teacher trying to get the attention of a classroom of bored teenagers.

"Who *is* that?" she asked, momentarily enthralled enough by the odd scene in front of her to forget her desire to turn around and go home.

"That's Smee." He rolled his eyes and then added, "*Captain* Smee."

"*Smee* is the captain?" From what she'd read and heard, and based on what she was witnessing now, Smee seemed an unlikely choice for captain.

Jax shrugged. "He's trying, but the pirates don't really do much anymore. It must be pretty easy being captain of a ship that never goes anywhere."

"How did that even happen?"

Jax's face darkened. "It happened when he murdered two of the Lost Boys."

She cringed. "I'm sorry, Jax. But . . . isn't that how it works here? Pirates kill Lost Boys and you kill them."

"In the days of Hook, it was not murder, just killin'. We battled. We fought. When we lost our friends, it was for

Neverland! Hook understood the difference between killing in battle and just killin'. Smee doesn't."

She wasn't sure she understood, not entirely. Murder was murder and adults killing children seemed barbaric no matter the circumstances. "Why was this different? What happened?"

Jax turned his back on the pirate ship and spun to face her, his arms wide. "It was the day of the Great War between the pirates and the Lost Boys. A battle between good and evil!"

"To the death!" squeaked the small boy who had reassured her about the pirates.

"Pidge! I'm tellin' it!"

"But I want to help!"

Jax groaned. "Fine, you can help. But just *help*."

Pidge grinned. "It was a battle between good and evil." He pulled out a small knife and jumped into a wide-legged stance, aiming the knife at Jax. "To the DEATH!"

"Pidge!"

Angela laughed, sinking into the grass to watch the show as Pidge sulked and pulled his knife back. "Someone just tell it!"

Jax continued. "Hook *said* it was meant to be the ultimate battle between good and evil, but really it was about the feud between Hook and Peter."

"And to get Peter's kids back!" Pidge chimed in, and Jax nodded.

"The pirates were no match for us." Jax swung his sword toward Pidge, stepping left, then stepping right. Pidge lifted his (much smaller) knife and jumped back to avoid Jax's blade.

"We defeated them in hours!" Pidge lunged forward toward Jax.

"Minutes!" came a voice from the crowd of Lost Boys.

"Seconds!"

Jax stopped his swordplay and looked at the crowd. "Now don't be ridiculous."

Angela giggled and Jax continued. "The pirates were defeated, embarrassed, and shamed. Pan's children were safe, but Hook would not stop. Driven by his hatred for Peter, he kept fighting. But he was old and no match for the great Peter Pan!" The boys cheered. "The pirates watched as their beloved Captain James Hook was defeated by his mortal enemy."

"And the crocodile!" Pidge opened his mouth and moaned as he leaned toward Jax, baring his teeth.

"The crocodile statue *fell* on him. It was still Peter that defeated him!"

Another boy called, "I bumped into that croc earlier in battle, I think I loosened it!"

"I gave it a nudge while they were fighting, I knew it was loose!"

"None of you liars touched the croc!" Jax yelled, aiming his sword at the group. "Pan defeated Hook and the pirates sulked from the deck of the ship." He took a deep breath, steadying his tone and lowering his voice. "But one pirate did not sulk. One sleazy—"

"Slimy!"

"—cowardly excuse for a pirate didn't care about Hook, he only wanted one thing . . . power."

"And gold!" a boy yelled.

"That's two things!" said another.

Jax lowered his voice and mumbled, "Obviously the gold would come with the power—would you quit interrupting me?" He straightened up. "Hook's very own first mate was stealing his gold and riches before the Great Captain was even defeated. He didn't even wait until the pirate was cold before moving in. His pockets heavy with Hook's treasures, he stumbled down the stairs to where the men had just watched their captain die."

"How do you know that?" a voice from the crowd asked skeptically.

"Know what?" Jax asked, his freckled cheeks red.

"That Smee had Hook's gold in his pockets. You weren't there."

"I saw him, Tank! He was loading up before the battle was even over, waddling around like a big ol' duck, pretending to help but really just waiting for the right moment to make his move. And when he realized Hook was gone, that's when he decided to do it. He ran up to the men, decked out in Hook's jewels and his coat, gripping Hook's pistol, and told them he was the captain now and it was time to show the Lost Boys that the pirates weren't beat!"

"I heard he shot someone," Pidge whispered. He'd come up beside Angela and she jumped at the sudden air in her ear. "Just up and shot someone to prove *he* was in charge."

Jax nodded solemnly. "More than one is what I heard. He was mad with power, desperate to show the men he was captain material. But good captains don't just shoot their men for no reason, and honorable captains don't kill you from behind. Hook was evil, no question, but he always practiced good form. But with Smee as captain, those days are gone."

"Now Neverland is even scarier," Pidge said quietly, the mood of the story shifting.

"What do you mean?" Angela whispered.

"Until you arrived, Neverland was missing its heart. It's like it knew Pan was never coming back, and that told the pirates he was never coming back. Their mood took over the island without Peter here to keep it alive. Neverland grew dark and the pirates grew more and more confident. When Peter found out Smee was captain, and what he'd done, he told us to stop fighting . . . that Smee was a different kind of enemy than Hook."

"So what happened? What did he do?" She realized now that her mother had told her this story, based on what her Grandpa Peter told her before he died. He hadn't been there of course, but the Lost Boys had filled him in on one of his trips back—probably much like they were doing now. But it was different hearing it here where it had actually happened, from the boys who had lived it. She could feel Neverland tense up under her, and she could feel the boys shiver as one as they approached the next part of the story. She pulled her sweater tighter despite the warmth of the suns.

"We'd just said goodbye to Peter," Jax continued softly, "when it happened. He had barely cleared the clouds when we heard it. A small gasp, and then a thud followed by another. By the time we turned around, two of our boys were on the ground, sliced along the neck, and the pirate that had done it was already halfway back to the man who had given the order—Smee."

"What did you do?" she whispered as the boys bowed their heads in memory of their fallen friends.

"We ran. The pirates had never killed like that outside of a battle or a mission. We didn't know what to do, so we retreated." He bowed his head, his cheeks red with shame.

"As we ran away, we heard 'im."

"Heard who?" she asked.

"Smee," Jax said. "Yelling at us from the ship. Shooting Hook's pistol into the air he said, 'Your nightmares did not die with Captain Hook! Never turn your back on me, Lost Boys! Never turn your back on Smee!'"

"And that's how Smee became captain," Pidge said from beside her.

"Wow," she breathed. "You were right. He murdered those boys. And his men." She shuddered. What had she gotten herself into, coming to Neverland?

"And he keeps doing it," Jax said. "We haven't battled the pirates in a long time, but we still hear gunshots coming from the ship sometimes."

"He kills his own men to show them he's in charge," the boy named Tank added, shaking his head at the thought.

"Hook didn't do that?" she asked.

"They'd always done *something* to deserve it. It might not have been a lot, but he always had a reason. Not like Smee. Smee kills because he's scared of losing control. And he'd send his men onto the island to hunt us just to show us that Neverland belonged to the pirates. But *he* doesn't do anything. Just sits around and drinks all day."

"So why do the men follow him?"

"Because they have to have a captain."

"Why don't they rebel?"

The boys looked at each other and shrugged. "That's not how the game works."

Somehow, their Lost Boy logic made sense. "And you want *me* to fight him now?"

"Peter told us to stay away, but Peter is gone now. You're here and Neverland knows it. We finally have a chance to take Neverland back. Smee was always afraid of Peter. Maybe he'll be afraid of you too."

"Maybe," she whispered as she watched the activity on the ship, but she doubted it. She wasn't Pan. She was a scrawny, thirteen-year-old girl, who couldn't fly or fight. But that man murdered children. He'd terrorized the boys her great-grandpa cared about so much. He'd forced them to hide in the world that had been Pan's home for so many years. Grandpa Peter would be crushed to know how they'd been living. Her mom would be crushed.

And she *was* in Neverland, after all . . . a little adventure couldn't hurt. "Do you think they're trying to go somewhere now? Maybe they're going to retreat?"

"Don't think so. They won't leave the lagoon without a fight. Smee is not a great captain, but he's stubborn and he likes his cushy life the way it is. We need to get closer to hear what they're saying." He motioned with his eyebrows to his right. "There's a trail down the side of the hill that leads to the entrance of the cave. There are rocks to hide behind and we'll be able to hear what they're saying."

Before she could protest getting closer to the man they'd

all just described as murderous and unpredictable, Jax was on his way and the boys were forming a single line behind him, making their way down the narrow path. Angela was left to bring up the rear.

CHAPTER 3

J ax was right. Hidden behind large boulders at the mouth of the cave, they could hear everything happening on the ship. The cave acted as a speaker, the sounds from the ship disappearing into its depths, then back out to bounce and echo around them. Angela felt like she was watching a pirate movie, not participating in a poorly planned, last-minute raid with kids her age against adults armed with guns and cannons.

Jax had been right about another thing—they were definitely not planning a retreat. Smee was screaming orders, but they were about defending the ship, not preparing it for departure.

"Load the cannons! Prep the rifles! Arm yourselves! Pan could be here at any moment and we must be ready!"

But Smee's shaky voice revealed the uncertainty that his barked orders tried to hide.

"They think Pan is back," she whispered, not sure if their voices would carry to the ship like the pirate voices carried to them.

Jax nodded, unsurprised. "This is Pan's Neverland." He motioned around them. "The only time it feels like this is when Pan is home."

"So . . . my arrival tipped them off. What will they do when they find out it's not Pan?"

Jax just shook his head.

"Well, we can't just raid the ship, they're expecting that." She hoped Jax didn't recognize the relief in her voice at the thought of putting off a pirate attack.

"You're right," he said. "They *are* expecting an attack . . . from Pan." At these last words, he turned to face her and lifted his eyebrows, a grin breaking out across his freckled and thus-far-serious face. She didn't like what that grin insinuated.

She turned her back on the pirate ship and sat in the dirt, leaning against the rock that was hiding them. "But what am I supposed to do, Jax?" After hearing what Smee had done to those two boys, she didn't feel like she could refuse a confrontation, but there was still the question of her experience. "I don't know the first thing about fighting pirates."

But even as she said it, she knew it wasn't true. She'd grown up with a Pan expert who used her as a sounding board for ideas and drafts. She probably knew more about Pan's fighting experience, his exploits, and his cleverness than even the boys sitting in front of her. And then something clicked in the back of her mind—a Pan plan that involved outsmarting pirates, *not* fighting them. She lifted her knees and leaned forward, resting one elbow on each. She looked up to see Jax grinning at her. He must have seen something change in her face—he knew she had a plan. Well, she had the beginnings of one at least. He hissed toward the other rocks where the rest of the boys were hiding, and when they poked their heads up, he motioned for them to come over. As they had when she told the story of how she'd come to Neverland, they formed a circle around her, crossing their legs and leaning forward, ready to hear her plan.

It was hard to think with them all staring like that, but she turned and asked Jax, "Do you think they remember his *voice?*"

A few minutes and one rushed planning session later, Angela was perched on the highest rock at the edge of the cave, a spot she'd only managed to reach by climbing an extremely awkward, for her, Lost Boy ladder. It was the perfect perch for their plan as it offered maximum projection of her voice but was hidden by the leaves of a weeping willow-like tree bending down from the ledge above. The boys had all loved her plan, though she was currently questioning her own sanity. Why hadn't she tried harder to get home? She'd come to Neverland to prolong her life, not get killed on the first day.

But she did have to admit, the idea of spending her days relaxing on the edge of this cove or diving from these rocks into the clear waters was enough motivation to move forward with her crazy, Pan-inspired plan. Maybe the Lost Boys were already rubbing off on her, but the idea of playing in this lagoon strengthened her resolve. She was a Pan, after all.

"You've always been a fighter," her mom told her when they'd first received her diagnosis, "and you always will be." Angela nodded at her mom across the span of worlds. She was ready. She was meant for this life. She was strong and she didn't let small setbacks like pirates or cancer keep her from what she wanted.

She looked down to where the boys were all waiting, spread out behind the spattering of rocks just inside the cave. A few took her glance as their cue, and they crawled off, heading to the other side of the lagoon to play their parts when it was their turn. The rest nodded their encouragement and Jax gave a signal that seemed to mean, "Get on with it."

She cleared her throat and braced herself on the boulder. She squared her shoulders and channeled the feelings that surfaced every time her mother called her brave. She thought about all the times she'd felt like giving up but hadn't because her mother had taken her hand and reminded her of who she was, of who their family was, and how together they could get through anything. She lifted her chin like she did before every chemo session, heard her mother's voice echoing the word "fighter" off the cave walls, and let out the fiercest, boldest, strongest crow she could muster.

The crow had the desired effect. All activity aboard the ship ceased. The men paused their work and Smee fell quiet as dozens of eyes lifted to the skies. Despite all the preparation of their weapons, not a single pirate moved to use one against the phantom crow. They just stood, frozen in their last moments of a pan-free existence.

Angela took advantage of their hesitation and filled the silence. She had no idea what Peter would have sounded like when he was young, so she just had to count on the fact that the pirates did not remember.

"You *codfish* think you can arm yourselves against me?"

The pirates looked at each other, some glancing furtively at their weapons, wondering if they would do any good. Most stayed motionless, but Smee, braver than his appearance, actions, and general demeanor made him seem, stepped forward.

"And just *who* are you?"

"Don't you know me? Who else could bring Neverland back to life and cause the faces of your men to go white with fear?"

"But that's *impossible*," Smee practically whined, his whole body shaking. The men closest to him glanced at each other and shifted uncomfortably.

Angela just giggled, the sound bouncing off the cave walls and flying around the pirates like she could not.

"Yours is the voice of a child! Peter Pan grew into a man."

"Neverland is a magical place full of mysteries," she

replied, using magic to fight his logic. Who was to say that Neverland wouldn't return Pan's youth if he'd really desired it?

Smee raised an eyebrow at this and turned to the man closest to him with his silent question. The man just shrugged, and she laughed at his confusion. Smee prickled at being laughed at, his round face glowing red. He had a pistol gripped in his right hand but no one to aim it toward, so he waved it in the air. The men surrounding him gave him a wide berth.

"What do you want from us, *boy*?" Smee bounced on his tiptoes, shouting at nothing. Dressed in Hook's red coat that was a few sizes too long but tight around the midsection, he looked like a child pretending to be the captain of a pirate ship while his siblings refused to acknowledge his claim to the role.

"I want my lagoon back."

"*Your* lagoon? We have claimed this spot in the name of the *Jolly Roger*. It is *my* lagoon now." He stomped his foot.

She giggled again. What was with this guy? "All of Neverland belongs to Pan."

"Pan deserted Neverland. He left the Lost Boys alone, made them run and hide and cower in fear. I, Captain Smee, killed two of your Lost Boys on my first day as captain. Neverland belongs to the grownups now, little boy."

She noticed Smee was now addressing her as though she were Pan. While his words would have been enough to make any child tremble and cry, she tried to see them as Pan would have seen them, as a challenge. To a young Pan, the fallen Lost Boys would have been the spoils of war and he would not have let their deaths bring him down. In fact, in his youth, Angela didn't think he even noticed when Lost Boys fell at the hands of the pirates. It was only as an adult, as a father returned to Neverland to save his children, that he began to see the Lost Boys as boys and not just part of his game.

Her pause had given Smee time to gain more confidence. He seemed pretty cocky talking to empty air. "I think you're a liar. An impostor. A sad Lost Boy trying to fill the void left by Pan. You're not even flying. You're a coward."

This putz was smarter than he looked, but his words were the fire she needed to push forward. "A coward, Smee? *You* are the coward who kills children from behind. *You* are the cowardly captain of a stationary ship! Your men don't fear you, they pity you! Just look at them!"

Smee spun around to face the men behind him. They jumped at the movement, but when he studied their faces for genuine fear, his face fell and his shoulders dropped. She'd hit a nerve. Before he could gear himself up for another tantrum, she spoke again.

"You want to see Pan fly? You want *me* to prove who *I* am because *you* have not proved yourself worthy as a captain? Fine. But don't blink, Smee. I am young, Neverland is back, and I am ready to PLAY."

The Lost Boys scattered, taking the cue. In the order they'd discussed, each let out a Pan-worthy crow that bounced off the blue water, up into the pirate ship, and danced like a fairy through the ears of the pirates. Before one crow faded out, another began. She didn't know if science supported the way their voices carried, but Neverland sure seemed to.

The pirates threw their arms over their heads and hit the deck, and Smee's brave face of only moments before faltered and fell. He tried to search the skies but was also fumbling with the pistol in his hand.

Angela let the ruckus die down and called, "This is my cove, you codfish. All of Neverland knows it."

The boys let out another round of crows, cementing the vision of Pan circling their ship in the heads of every pirate on board. When the round faded, they initiated the next part of the plan.

The chants started as a low rumble and slowly grew louder. A few pirates dared to come to the edge of the ship, leaning over the rail to hear better. From the trees and rocks and grasses surrounding the lagoon, one word emerged, over, and over, gaining volume as it bounced through the cove.

"Pan . . . Pan . . . Pan! Pan! Pan!"

While most of the boys chanted, a few others ran through the trees surrounding them and riled the animals nesting there. From the forest came the squawks of birds and the grunts of other sleepy Never-creatures now disturbed from their slumber.

The chanting was joined by a cacophony of wild noises, seeming to support the message the Lost Boys were spreading—Pan was back and all of Neverland agreed.

And then, Neverland offered its own surprise. Breaks in the still waters revealed one head after another, and the splashes of the mermaids once driven to the bottom of the lagoon joined the chaos around them. Angela laughed, thrilled by their appearance.

"Pan! Pan! Pan!" The mermaids splashed around, flipping their tails and jumping toward the ship, clearly eager to rid their home of this monstrosity.

As the chanting continued, Angela drove home her final point. "My Neverland has spoken! You are not welcome here, Smee!"

"Captain Smee! It's *Captain* Smee!" He seemed to speak more to himself than anyone else as he ducked behind a barrel, hiding from an invisible threat. But his crew and his ship had not waited for his orders to make their next move. The men were pulling up anchors and lifting sails and aiming the rudders of the ship toward the channel that led into the ocean.

Smee stepped out from his hiding place and gathered himself. "Weigh anchor! Sail on, men!"

As the bow of the ship turned toward the channel and began to make its way out of the cove, Smee ran toward the stern of the ship, screaming toward the sky.

"This isn't over, Pan! You've not heard the last of Captain Smee!"

***

The great ship broke free of the channel and emerged into open water, but the pirate named Lamont wasn't watching the scene they were leaving behind. He was watching Smee. The captain was standing at the stern of the ship, gripping the rail and staring back at the lagoon they'd just abandoned. From where Lamont was watching, far enough to be out of shooting range but close enough to observe Smee's reaction to recent events, the observing pirate could tell Smee was sore. Sore at Pan's insults, sore at the loss of his leisurely captain's life in the lagoon, but even more sore about the whooping and the cheering and the dancing happening on the shores lining that lagoon. Smee stared down into the waters, Lamont following his gaze, and watched Lost Boy after Lost Boy emerge from their hiding spots and join those already celebrating, throwing their heads back and crowing over their victory.

Smee looked to the sky, and Lamont knew he was preparing to see the thin, lithe form of a boy of ten or eleven lower gracefully from above and land gently among his Lost Boys. But the pirate knew that's not what Smee would see. Instead, the Lost Boys gathered around a large rock at the entrance to the lagoon's cave. They were looking up, not to the skies, but to the top of a giant boulder. The pirate watched Smee squint. They were cheering and applauding a form not floating through the air around them but standing on the top of that boulder. Smee glanced behind him at a few of his crew who were watching the same scene, also about to experience the same realization, the thing Lamont already knew; it was not *Pan* who had driven them from the lagoon. Smee turned back to the boys, straining against the edge of the ship, leaning over to catch a glimpse of the object of the boys' admiration. As a warm breeze picked up off the water and made its way into the lagoon, it pushed aside the branches falling over the rock, the branches that were creating a protective curtain around the impostor. As the curtain parted, the pirate, the crew, and Smee could see a child of twelve or maybe older, but it was not Pan or even a Lost Boy—it was something Neverland and the pirates had not seen since the days of Wendy. It was a *girl*. Lamont smiled as he watched her raise her hands in celebration, but Smee whirled around and the men watching the scene with him scattered. He still had his gun in his hand, and he'd been known to randomly shoot when upset . . . and he was clearly upset.

He pointed the pistol at a pirate close to him and the man put his hands in the air.

"Who *is* that?" Smee bellowed, waving the gun toward the lagoon and then back at the pirate.

The man just shook his head, afraid to speak.

Smee let out a guttural groan of frustration and charged at the man in front of him, shoving him over the barrel set behind him. The barrel fell with the man but didn't crack or burst; it just rolled around the deck uselessly, which infuriated Smee even more. He clenched his free fist, raised his pistol toward the sky, and shot.

"Men!" He stomped his foot, and as he did, a body hit the deck next to him with a satisfying crack. He'd hit one of the men perched in the crow's nest of the ship. Smee shrugged and kicked the body, yelling again. "Everyone get down here, now! *Now* I say, you dirty, disgusting excuses for pirates."

He ran to the stern of the ship and called to the men still scattered about, then stomped to the center, calling to the men manning the sails. "Gather 'round, ya scurvy dogs, or I will search this ship and shoot every pirate I find and then shoot the rest of you for sport! We've been outsmarted by a GIRL! You useless turds let us get tricked by a girl!"

As the men congregated, he continued to pace, tramping across the deck, his chest rising and falling heavily, his round cheeks and bulbous nose flushed tomato red. His men were gathering—slowly, but they were gathering—and Lamont watched as Smee tried to control his breathing so he could speak. It was only this morning that the captain had been sprawled out on the bow of the ship, drunk as a skunk, basking in the quiet gloom of a Pan-free Neverland, just as he'd been for years. Lamont, observing from the shadows, just as *he'd* been doing for years, heard Smee's groan of rage as the clouds had parted and the sun shone on Neverland for the first time in ages. Smee stood on unsteady feet, squinting against the bright sun. He'd lifted his gaze to the sky, his eyes darting among the newly white, puffy clouds, and bellowed one word. "Pan!"

Lamont heard the name he'd hoped would never again be uttered in Neverland; he'd seen the clouds clear and panic wash over Smee's face and knew. He knew it wouldn't be long before he had to emerge from the shadows and break free of the anonymity he'd built over the years.

As the men waited on the deck, Smee climbed to the helm, trying to pull himself together and salvage a little bit of dignity. As he straightened, some men were gazing longingly back at the lagoon or fidgeting toward the barrels of rum stacked up behind them. No one looked like they expected much from this meeting. They'd been inactive for so many years, under Smee's orders, that none of them seemed to believe anything would actually come from this turn of events. But Lamont knew things were about to change and change drastically.

"Men! This insult will not stand! That was not Pan forcing us out of our lagoon but a fraud! I will not let our peaceful lives be interrupted by a Peter Pan impostor trying to bring back their 'good ol' days.' I will not be tormented by *a child* like our former captain was. Times have changed and it's all thanks to Captain Smee of the *Jolly Roger*." There was mumbling from the men, but it was hard to tell if it was in agreement or doubt. Smee continued, "This wasn't just a Lost Boy! This was a *girl*! We must act!"

"What would ye have us do, Captain?" someone called, and Smee rolled his eyes. These men were trained to take orders, not think for themselves, and for years that had sat well with Smee, but now he needed help.

"Who *is* she!?" he practically yelped. "This girl impersonating Pan who has brought Neverland back to life?" Smee rubbed his temples, and Lamont waited for the memories to make their way through the cloud of rum Smee had lived under for so many years. As Smee thought, he plopped down where he stood and crossed his legs. He set his elbows on his knees and rested his chin in his hands. Lamont stood straighter. It wouldn't be long before Smee remembered. He was an inept and lazy captain, but he'd once been Hook's first mate, and most of Hook's best ideas had come from Smee. Lamont had seen what Smee was capable of when he wasn't drowning in rum.

Smee was mumbling now, repeating his own words, "She brought Neverland back to life . . . Only Pan can do that . . . The brat said it herself, 'Who else could bring Neverland back to life?' Who else indeed?"

Lamont watched Smee's eyes begin to sparkle behind

the blanket of humiliation and drink, and the pirate knew he was remembering events and information from many years ago. Remembering that the Pan name did not die when Pan left Neverland. He'd had children. And those children had restored Neverland just as Pan had before them.

Smee jumped up from his spot and pointed back toward the lagoon. He had it. "That is not Pan! That is a *descendant* of Pan! A descendant who still believes." He groaned.

Now Smee was remembering the steps he'd taken to prevent this day from coming . . . but did he remember Lamont? Neverland tended to blur the past if you let it (and most people did), and the amount of rum he'd consumed over the years was bound to make his memory even fuzzier, but he was looking around as though he remembered *something* . . . talking to *someone*.

"She must be stopped, men! The Lost Boys are fighting again, Neverland is bright and lush, and this is no life for a pirate! What do we do? How do we get rid of her?"

It was time. The pirate couldn't wait for Smee to remember him; he would have to make himself known. If Lamont let him continue on this route, Smee would concoct a plan to attack and kill . . . and he would not have that. His years of blending into the background, of avoiding Smee while still keeping a close eye on him, were orchestrated specifically to keep that from happening. But those days were gone. It was time to take action.

He cleared his throat loudly and waited. Smee looked up and Lamont made eye contact with his captain for the first time in thirteen years.

Lamont stepped forward. "I think I can help."

CHAPTER 4

The boys were still chanting, "Pan! Pan! Pan!" as the pirate ship made its way down the channel, toward the ocean, and away from the cove. They were whooping and cheering around the rock on which she stood, celebrating their first victory in years, but Angela suddenly didn't feel much like celebrating. She'd just done something so Pan-like, so fitting of her heritage, that no one, including these boys dancing around her, could possibly understand what a moment that was for a girl who was supposed to be weak and dying. No one except her mother.

The moment the first sail had risen and the ship had shown the first sign of movement, she'd wanted to turn to her, throw her arms around her, and jump up and down like they had every time they'd won a hard-earned victory. Like when Moira had landed her first publishing contract after years of fighting with agents and critics. Like when Angela had *finally* passed her math class.

"Life is one big battle," her mom always told her. "You have to be willing to fight for what you want." And today, Angela had fought and won. She could see her mother smiling and whispering, "That's my girl," but the image in her mind couldn't hug her or stroke her hair, and that made the victory a little less fulfilling and the time she would spend in Neverland a little more depressing.

After a few minutes of celebration, with the ship back in open water where it belonged, the boys seemed to forget she was there as they got reacquainted with their lagoon, splashing in the water and jumping off rocks into the blue pool. Their indifference to her presence suited her just fine. She slid down off her perch into the sand below, brushed off her green joggers, and climbed the trail they'd hiked down into the lagoon, back up to the top of the hill where she could watch the festivities below without taking part in them. This would have bothered her mom. Angela liked being alone more than she liked being even with her closest friends, and that worried her. *"Join in the fun, sweetie,"* she could hear her mom whisper. *"You deserve this."* But the sound of the voice in her head, rather than bolster her courage like it had during her adventure, pricked at her heart and brought tears to her eyes.

Great, she thought as she sniffled, her first full day in Neverland and she was already crying. The suns were setting over the ocean, turning the lagoon from bright blue to orange, and she wondered what her mom was doing without her. She was probably making a pot of decaf tea and turning on their favorite record, settling in for a quiet evening of reading. The house would be warm with candlelight and filled with the smell of peppermint. The thought brought a sob out of her throat.

"Lady Pan? Why are you crying?"

She jumped at Jax's voice and sniffed hard, trying to pull back all the liquid that was making its way down her face with one pull of air. It was useless, though. He'd seen. This boy she barely knew had seen her crying when he already had a hard time believing she measured up to the Pan he missed so dearly.

Ugh, whatever. There was nothing wrong with a good cry, and it was time these boys knew it.

She sniffled again. "How did you know to come find me?" The boys had been so wrapped up in their celebration, she didn't think anyone would notice she was gone.

Jax pointed to the sky she'd been admiring only moments before. The orange glow of the setting suns had faded to a charcoal gray as the clouds moved in from the edges. A single raindrop pinged her head and she shivered.

"Neverland told me. Just like it's tied to Pan's arrivals and departures, it's also tied to his moods. Well, to your moods now."

"Wait," she said with another sniffle. "You're telling me I can control the weather?" Neverland was full of surprises, but this one could potentially be to her benefit. She wanted to be more excited about it but was having a hard time mustering enthusiasm about anything at the moment.

"Kind of." Jax said, sitting down next to her, "I mean, if you can control your emotions, you might be able to control the weather. Are you good at that?"

Angela squared her shoulders and dabbed at the corner of her eye with her sleeve. "Well"—she looked up at the sky and saw it had stopped sprinkling—"I've stopped crying now, haven't I?"

"True. So, why *were* you crying?"

She shrugged. "I'm just sad, that's all."

"Sad?"

"Yeah, sad. That feeling when your heart just sits in your stomach, making you feel sick and like you can't breathe and you feel like you want to throw up or throw something but also just curl up into a ball and sob until it dislodges itself. Ya know. *Sad.*" She probably wasn't making any sense to this boy who'd spent his life sleeping under the stars and having adventures, first with Peter Pan and then as the leader of the Lost Boys, but it was how she felt and he could deal with it.

To her surprise, though, he didn't cock his head in confusion. He sighed. "Oh. *That's* sad." He nodded. "I know that one."

She pulled her knees to her chest, wrapping her arms around them. "You do?"

"Yea, that's how I felt when Peter didn't come back. And when you told us he'd never be coming back. And I think I felt like that before I came to Neverland . . . or, when I first got to Neverland." He shrugged. "I know sad."

"Oh." She rested her chin on her knees, not knowing what else to say.

"But *why* are you sad? You defeated the pirates! The lagoon is ours!"

She sighed and whispered the words she knew so many Lost Boys had uttered before her. "I miss my mother."

"Oh."

As a blanket of darkness fell over them and her first day in Neverland drew to a close, the silence stretched on. Finally Angela had to break it. "So, you heard me when I said Pan was never coming back?"

He nodded slowly. "Yes, I heard you."

"But you said —"

"We pretend around here, it's what we do. And lately, pretending Pan will be back is our favorite game. I guess I wasn't done playing."

"Do you miss him a lot?"

Jax wrinkled his nose. "Sometimes."

"What do you mean?"

"Young Peter was our leader. He bossed us around and made us play his games. But the man Peter was nice. He was our friend and I miss *him*."

Angela nodded. A little growing up could do a lot for a person.

After a moment, he jumped as though something had surprised him and turned to look at her, his eyes wide. "But we don't have to pretend anymore."

"Why?" she asked.

"Because in a way, Pan *is* back."

As Angela smiled and the last of the day's sunlight broke through the now retreating clouds, she felt a little less like crying.

***

The moment Lamont had spoken, all eyes aboard the ship turned to him. He cleared his throat again nervously, almost regretting his decision to come forward and throw away the anonymity he'd worked so hard to cultivate over the last thirteen years.

He still had time. The captain didn't seem to recognize him, and if he let out a grunt and proposed a toast, Smee would have gladly drank with him, and he could have stepped back into the crowd and disappeared again. But he couldn't. The moment he'd heard "Pan's" voice in the air, he knew his days of anonymity were over.

"And just who are you, pirate?" Smee asked.

"Name's Lamont, sir. We've, uh, we've spoken before . . ."

Lamont watched Smee study him and mouth his name over and over as their conversation of many years past seemed to play out behind his eyes.

Smee had been lounging, as he always was in the days following Hook's demise and Pan's disappearance from Neverland, when he'd summoned Lamont to his side. The men were sure Smee cared about nothing but drinking, relaxing, wearing the gold and jewels he'd acquired from Hook, and every now and then going into the bars and meeting a woman or two. But he'd been worrying. Worrying that his peaceful existence would be interrupted at any moment. While his orders were few and far between, he had something he needed help with.

"You're one of the only men on this ship with any sense, Lamont. I need you to do something for me."

Lamont had not taken Smee's veiled compliment to heart. Knowing many of the other men on the ship, it didn't mean much, but he'd nodded for Smee to go on. All the pirates on board knew it was best to be agreeable when talking to Smee. He'd already proven himself a trigger-happy captain, so to avoid being shot, Lamont had been quick to agree to anything Smee asked him to do. If he'd known where it would lead, he probably would have taken his chances with the bullet.

"Pan's visits have ended. I don't think he'll be making any more trips into Neverland."

Lamont nodded again. It made sense. Time was hard to track here, but it had been a very long time since they'd seen Pan, and the last time they had he was old, gray, and slow. After so many years out of Neverland, time was catching up with him.

"That's a good thing, sir, no?" Lamont asked.

"Yes . . . yes . . . it's a good thing for now. But Pan had children. And who knows how far the Pan line extends. I'm sending you on a mission to find out. Find out if Pan's family still believes in Neverland, and if they do, take care of them, Lamont—by *any* means necessary. I am enjoying this quiet,

Pan-free existence and I would like it to continue. Now, go. And don't return without answers that will satisfy me." He'd patted the gun at his hip. "And if you fail, pirate, I will find you. This job will not go undone even if I have to finish it myself."

Now Lamont stood before Smee for the first time since being given his mission, or at least the first time Smee remembered. The conversation upon Lamont's return was one Lamont preferred to stay lodged in the deep, rum-soaked recesses of Smee's memory.

"Lamont," Smee now mumbled from his place in front of the gathered men. "Yes, Lamont. I remember. I gave you a very important job."

"Yes, sir."

"You told me you'd completed that job." He remembered. "Did you?"

"No, sir."

"It appears you lied to your captain, is that right?"

"Yes, sir."

Smee's right hand traveled down his side toward his pistol and the men around Lamont backed away to accommodate Smee's sometimes lousy aim.

"I should shoot you where you stand, Lamont. Pirates who don't follow my orders get shot. Did you know that?"

Every pirate on board knew that. "Yes, sir."

"So, why shouldn't I shoot you?"

Smee rarely asked questions before shooting. He seemed to be hoping that Lamont's mission had not been a complete failure. Lamont only hoped he would make it through this conversation alive.

"I can help, sir. With the girl. I can help get her out of here."

"This *girl*"—his gray mustache twitched—"she is a descendant of Pan, yes?"

Lamont swallowed. "Yes, sir."

"And you were meant to make sure none of his descendants could return to Neverland. You were supposed to take care of them. Did you do that?"

Lamont bowed his head, his face burning red with shame at Smee's words, but not because he'd disappointed his captain. "No, sir. I did not take care of them." The words set his insides on fire with guilt.

"Then why should I let you live, Lamont? How can you possibly help this situation? Just exactly who the hell do you think you are?"

Lamont breathed deeply. "I'm her father, sir."

***

It rained on Angela's first night in Neverland and she wondered if the other boys knew why, or even noticed. Lost Boy sleep, she soon learned, was the sleep of the dead. They kept themselves up well after exhaustion should have driven them to their beds, and when they could barely stand a moment longer, they collapsed. Some made it to their beds, some simply sat down where they stood, curled up, and began snoring. To someone who'd always slept in a nice warm bed under a down comforter, it was a sight to behold.

The stillness of the sleeping boys permeated the treehouse

until it was almost louder than the wildlife outside—the wildlife that had come alive as soon as the suns set. Angela's room was comfortable enough; in fact, it was the best room in the treehouse.

When they'd reached the Lost Boy's favorite hideout after their victory over the pirates, most of the boys scattered, either running off to play or sleep. The ones who stayed behind didn't seem to know what to do with the girl standing in the middle of their home. There'd been a moment of silence while Angela studied her surroundings and the boys tried to figure out where to put her.

There were even whispers of . . . "Does she need to sleep?"

"Of course, she needs to sleep! She's human, isn't she?"

In the middle of a wide expanse of dense trees in all shapes and varieties was a circular opening the size of a football field, in the middle of which sat a group of thick trees, with strong branches that provided support for the rooms that had been built haphazardly around them.

The house was a wonder of modern engineering, and she found herself thinking that if any of these boys ever wanted to go back to her world, they would have promising architecture careers ahead of them. There were different levels of rooms with stairs going up the trunk to each different floor, and between each tree was a rope bridge. But the most amazing thing about the treehouse was the fact that if you didn't know what you were looking at, you probably wouldn't notice it. Moss, grass, and leaves were draped over each room, and many were built under leaves that provided a natural curtain of protection.

Just outside the main entrance of the treehouse was a fire

pit, empty now, as the boys had been gone all day, with rocks and logs scattered around it as chairs. It looked exactly like the type of place the boys in her class would have loved to spend their time.

She was surveying the hideout, looking for somewhere she might be able to get some privacy when Pidge piped up.

"Wendy had a bed! You need a bed, right?"

"I mean . . . that would be nice," she said slowly. "Don't you . . ."

Jax jumped in. "We don't sleep much, so leaves and stuff are good for us, but it's OK. I know the perfect place."

The perfect place turned out to be a room they'd built just in case.

"No matter how many new hideouts we've built since Peter left, we always build a room for him."

The room for Peter was in the center of the tree and circled the trunk. And it had, thank goodness, a bed . . . of sorts.

"It's just a lot of old pillowcases and clothes that Wendy sewed together and we stuffed with leaves and grass, but Peter seemed to like it."

When they'd entered the room, Angela had barely been able to stand from exhaustion, and would have been happy to lie on her sweater in the dirt if it meant getting a little sleep.

"Thank you," she'd whispered, and each boy bellowed, "Good night!" as they'd left her to go to their rooms or to continue their games.

The bed was comfortable enough and Angela was exhausted, but despite her hopes that sleep would come quickly, she was restless. After a short time, the treehouse was silent but the woods surrounding it were not. Maybe it was the noise of night in Neverland that made the boys run themselves into a coma before they slept, because with every howl, every chirp, every call of a bird and exchange of creature conversation, Angela jumped. And the longer she was awake, the more she missed home. And the more she missed home, the mistier her eyes became and the heavier the air grew around her until the pace of the drops hitting the roof of the treehouse matched the speed of the tears sliding down her cheeks.

It was only when the drum of the raindrops drowned out the cacophony of nightlife outside that she fell into a deep, dreamless sleep.

***

"So, you're Pidge and you're Tank?"

Tank nodded, and the one called Pidge jumped, trying to reach Tank's height. "Yup!"

"Right," she said, not feeling very accomplished. Both Pidge, with his pointed bottom lip and thin arms, and Tank, who was built just as his name suggested, were easy to remember.

She turned to another boy. "And you're . . ." She tried desperately to recall Jax's voice as he'd pointed out each boy from their spot at the top of the hill the night before. But he'd gone so fast, clearly not agreeing that it was important she knew everyone's name.

She shrugged, giving up.

"I'm Dot!"

"Oh, yea." It didn't help that their names were kind of ridiculous.

The morning after Angela's first night was clear and fresh, and she'd risen from her bed, her eyes dry and her determination strong. She wouldn't spend her days in Neverland crying for her mother. If she couldn't get home, she would try to make the most of her time in this magical land.

Now, they were standing on the sandy edges of the lagoon the morning after the pirate coup—or maybe it was already afternoon. Time did funny things in Neverland, but it didn't really matter when you had forever.

She plopped down in the sand between Pidge and Jax. Jax was watching the water rather than paying attention to their name game.

"I guess I've got all the time I need to learn them all," she said to no one in particular, which was good because no one in particular was really listening to her. Some were splashing on the edge of the water, some were sunning themselves, and some were playing a risky version of tag that involved swords.

She leaned back on her elbows to watch them play, the bare skin of her arms resting in the warm sand, her heavy sweater discarded in the sand behind her. The Lost Boys were a bit of a mystery to her, and she imagined they always would be, this group of boys who chose to leave their homes and spend eternity as children. They didn't seem as obsessed with the idea of a mother as past stories had suggested, and she wondered if Wendy's attempts to domesticate them, and her success at finding some of their earlier counterparts' homes, had cured them of that. In fact, most of them besides Pidge, Jax, and Tank, seemed fairly indifferent about her presence in Neverland. She tried not to be hurt. She wouldn't make much of a mother anyway.

She was fascinated by the little one named Pidge, who seemed to have taken that role on himself. As the boys acted out elaborate games of make-believe, Lost Boys vs. Pirates or Lost Boys vs. Great Beasts of Neverland, Pidge ran behind, comforting anyone who fell or pulling them (well, pretending to pull them) out of harm's way until they were well again. He was the same one who had been so concerned about her lack of desire to fight the pirates, and she wondered what made him so gentle while the other boys were so . . . wild.

She turned to Jax, who sat next to her on the beach, and found him gazing intently into the water in front of him. She looked out to where he was staring. The waters were blue and still, so she couldn't understand what he was studying with such focus.

"Earth to Jax! What are you staring at?"

He didn't even blink as he answered, "There's gonna be mermaid trouble."

"Mermaids?" She sat up and looked harder into the water.

"Mermaids!?" Pidge yelped, clearly less excited than she was.

She hadn't seen the mermaids again since they'd helped get them the lagoon back. Once they'd accomplished their goal, they disappeared back into the water and she'd hoped she would get a chance to thank them for their help, but they stayed hidden.

"They don't really want us here," Jax had told her after she'd asked when they might see them. "If we see them again, it won't be to exchange pleasantries."

"Aw, c'mon. They helped us get the lagoon back. That's gotta mean something."

"They wanted the lagoon back for themselves. That's the only reason they helped. The mermaids are pretty selfish."

Angela doubted they were any more selfish than a group of adolescent boys whose sole purpose in life was to never grow up and always have fun, but she kept that to herself.

No matter how much she'd pressed, it was unanimous—they didn't want the mermaids to show themselves.

But now it seemed they would, and despite the warnings, she couldn't even pretend to hide her excitement. Her legs still spread out in front of her, her bare feet just at the edge of the water, she placed a hand over her eyes to block the sun and get a better view. Was that a shadow? But before she could continue to wonder, she heard Jax and Pidge give an "uh-oh!" from either side of her, and there was a tug on her leg and her butt was dragging through the sand, her feet disappearing into the water, giving her just enough time to take a big gulp of air before the rest of her body followed.

For many terrifying moments, she was being pulled into the water, deeper and deeper, and when she struggled to get back to the top, the pull became stronger. She opened her eyes, determined to get a glimpse of what was wrapped around her ankle, and it took all she had not to gasp and let a mouthful of water into her lungs. She was being pulled into an underwater city. Logs, driftwood, and giant clam shells formed houses, held together with rope made of seaweed, and paths were forged like roads through walls of seagrass. She looked down and a woman with mossy green hair and a bra of what appeared to be algae had a strong grip on her foot. She was not the mystical, beautiful creature Angela had always imagined when her mother mentioned the mermaids of the lagoon. Her skin was tinted green and her fingernails were long and sharp, digging into Angela's ankle. Her features were angled and her teeth came to razor-edged points as she grinned up at Angela, pulling her deeper and deeper.

Anger burned in Angela's chest, or maybe it was her lungs desperate for air, and she didn't know what this chick thought was going to happen, but she was not going to be a ploy in whatever this game against the Lost Boys was. Angela had come here hoping Neverland would save her life, not threaten it at every turn. As the mermaid laughed, delighted at this new game, Angela's face must have mirrored her mom's when Angela talked back, because for just a second the mermaid's grip loosened.

Angela took advantage of the moment and kicked hard. The mermaid's mouth formed into an "Oh!" and a surge of bubbles shot out as she pulled her hand back. Angela didn't hang around to see just how mad mermaids could get. She kicked again, this time with both feet, and used her arms to propel her up. Cool air met her lungs as her head broke the surface. She breathed deep as she kicked to stay afloat and to push toward shore before someone tried to grab at her again. As she kicked, she realized she was surrounded by Lost Boys, treading water and staring at her. She crawled up onto the sand, panting, and turned back toward the water now dotted with the heads of the boys.

"What?" she gasped, trying to catch her breath as she leaned over onto her knees. They didn't seem very relieved to see her alive.

"We were coming to rescue you," Jax said, looking from Angela back down to the water.

"But you . . . you . . ." Pidge seemed just as confused as Jax.

"What?" she said. "Rescued myself?"

"Well, yea . . . " Tank added.

She shrugged. "You were too slow, I guess. Now you better get back up here before I need to rescue you!"

The boys scrambled to shore, still looking sore that their rescue mission had been unsuccessful. But honestly, how long did they think she could hold her breath? If she'd waited for them to come to rescue her, she'd probably be passed out on the bottom of the lagoon. It was like her mom said, "You need to learn to take care of yourself, because no one else is going to do it." She said this the most after Angela asked questions about her long-absent father, and she never let Angela forget that he'd left before Angela was born and had never once taken care of them.

All the boys were back on land except Pidge, who was slower and smaller than the rest. He was crawling up the shallow slope toward the sandy shore when Angela noticed a familiar shadow creeping toward his feet. She jumped forward and grabbed him under the shoulders, pulling him the rest of the way up to the sand just as a hand with long, sharp fingernails broke the surface of the water.

"Hey!" Angela yelled as she tossed Pidge into the sand behind her and stepped toward the edge of the water. "You! With the moldy hair!" The top of a head and a pair of eyes appeared above the water like an enchanting crocodile ready for an attack. "*What* is your problem?"

The eyes looked from Angela to the boys and narrowed, but there was no response. Angela didn't even know if the mermaid spoke English, but she knew a bully when she saw one and she was done being bullied. She stepped closer to the edge and could hear the boys murmuring behind her, but she wasn't afraid. Bullies only responded to strength.

The mermaid lifted her head a little farther out of the water and regarded Angela with icy blue eyes. "You speak strange words, girl." The mermaid's voice was high, almost a screech, and Angela cringed in spite of herself. "This is *our* home, it is not a play yard."

"What do you mean?" Angela asked.

"Just what I said. For years these boys have been using our home as a playground, the home that has belonged to us since the dawn of Neverland."

Angela looked back at Jax and he shrugged. Angela groaned inwardly. They were the intruders, *not* the mermaids. She looked back at the mermaid, her mind trying to work toward a solution that wouldn't end in constant attempts at drowning.

"Well, it's a home *we* helped you get back from the pirates."

"That does not give you the right to take it over and use it for your silly games."

She seemed to forget it was one of those silly games that

had run the pirates out in the first place, but still, she was right. She was a snot, but she was right.

"Well"—Angela placed her hands on her hips—"the pirates would still be parked here if it weren't for us, so I think that deserves something. This is a big lagoon, can't we share?"

Jax stepped up beside her and elbowed her side. Apparently, Lost Boys didn't share. Well, it was time they learned. She elbowed him back and stepped closer to the edge of the water.

"Share?" the mermaid said slowly.

"Yes. When we come to play in the lagoon, we will stay on this half of the beach and the water. This side of the cave." She pointed to the cave to her left. "We won't stay all the time, but when we're here, we just ask for a small section in return for freeing *your* home"—she glared at Jax—"from the pirates."

Without a word, her head disappeared below the surface. Angela didn't move, as she imagined she was conferring with the other mermaids.

"What are you doing?" Jax asked.

"Look," she said, "she's right. We can't just take over their home because we want a place to play. Who are we, Columbus?"

Jax raised an eyebrow.

"Never mind," she said. "It's just not right. There are plenty of other places to play around here."

"But this is the best spot!"

The mermaid returned, and Angela and Jax both turned to her.

"You have a deal, girl."

"Great, thank you. But my name is Ang—"

But before she could finish, the mermaid was gone.

***

"That was great!" Pidge chirped from beside Angela. He'd become her new best friend since his rescue, and as they trekked from the lagoon toward the treehouse, he stayed by Angela's side. She'd decided it would be wise to show the mermaids they were serious about their deal by hanging out somewhere else for the next few days.

"Well, I've dealt with plenty of mean girls in my life. She's just a mean girl with a fin. They were the worst when my hair started to fall out and ... "

She stopped walking and reached up to touch her short, soft curls. She remembered the days of chemo and how she was so exhausted and sick she could barely move but was still fighting to go to school and be normal. The girls were terrible, but her mother told her she had to work for what she wanted, and if she wanted to go to school, she'd need to fight back against anyone who stood in her way.

She remembered the days after chemo when she was pushing herself to act normal, but she was losing so much weight, her clothes were hanging off her body, and she could barely talk without gasping for air, and everywhere she went, the girls in her grade stared. They didn't make fun outright—no one would obviously make fun of the cancer kid—but they whispered. And they ignored her. And they giggled. The giggling was the worst. They jumped whenever she coughed, like they could catch what she had, and no one sat with her at lunch and some even mocked her from across the room. When she stopped going to school, her mom's face told her she thought she hadn't fought back hard enough, even though her arms welcomed her home.

But as she stood there in the grass under the warm sun, she wasn't thinking about the glares from the girls; she was thinking about the body they had been glaring at. Because when Angela looked down, she wasn't looking at *that* body; she was looking at her pre-cancer body. She'd never been very . . . curvy, but before cancer, her arms had a little bit of muscle from doing yoga with her mom, and she had enough meat on her bones to keep them from protruding out at the shoulder blades or her knees, but after? After cancer, you could see every bone, every tendon. Her body ate away at her muscle, and her arms looked as though they would snap if you pulled too hard.

But now? Now she was herself. She hadn't noticed among all the pirate and mermaid drama, but her once pale skin had soaked in the suns and was bronzed and glowing, and her thighs rounded out past her knees instead of just making her legs long knobby sticks with absolutely no definition. In Neverland, she'd been walking and running and jumping and yelling and hadn't once gotten winded. She hadn't had a nosebleed since home. The only indication that she'd once been sick was her hair, still growing back after chemo had taken it, and the inhaler she'd had in her pocket for those moments back home when she couldn't seem to catch her breath.

"What's wrong, Lady Pan?"

Pidge had noticed she was no longer beside him and had turned around to come see why she'd stopped walking. He saw she was staring down at her body, so he looked too but didn't seem to see anything worth looking at.

What was wrong? she thought. Technically nothing. Technically, everything was exactly right, and her mom's plan had worked exactly the way she'd hoped; Neverland had made her better. Her stomach clenched and she felt like she'd swallowed a rock. Her mom was right, she was better . . . and if she wanted to stay that way, she could never go home.

But Pidge was waiting for an answer, and she had no idea how to explain the rush of feelings that had just overcome her.

She looked up and offered a small smile. "Nothing, Pidge. Absolutely nothing is wrong."

CHAPTER 5

"L ady . . . wait! Lady P—hey!"

She could hear Jax struggling to keep up with her as she ducked and swerved and crawled through the wooden corridors that led to the top of the Lost Boys treehouse hideout. Only a few days ago, the sight of ladders and stairways and small spaces to climb through and beds suspended in the air would have made her nauseous. In fact, just days ago everything made her nauseous. And tired. And winded. But today, she felt great, and from the moment she'd noticed how great she felt, she hadn't stopped moving. It was partially taking advantage of her new body, partially trying to outrun the truth about her new existence, but either way, she was on the move.

With Jax hot on her heels, she emerged onto the flat roof of the treehouse, climbing up and standing on the boards that were surprisingly sturdy, considering they'd been built by kids. With her hands on her hips, she looked around at the rolling hills of green against the bright blue sky. From this spot in the fort, she could see for miles, and for the first time since her arrival, she really noticed how Neverland almost seemed to be dozens of climates shoved together on one island. In the distance, towering above the forests surrounding them, were snow-covered, jagged mountains. But to her immediate right and left, the soft hills resembled pictures she'd seen of Ireland, complete with gently flowing streams carving their way through the dirt and grass. A rainbow still shimmered over the water in the distance, and as Angela watched, she could have sworn she saw a flamingo dancing under its arc. Neverland was a world built from the dreams of children, so she supposed anything was possible. As she surveyed the land, she breathed in the fresh, cool air. This was why her mother had sent her here.

"Lady Pan." Jax was panting when he emerged just a few seconds behind her, "What . . . what are you doing?"

"I'm playing, Jax. What does it look like?" She picked up a ball rolling on the ground beside her and gave it a few dribbles. Sports weren't really her thing, but if playing was what you did in Neverland, she'd give it a try.

"You feel better, then?" he asked, and she raised an eyebrow. He hadn't understood when she said she was sick. "You're not sad?"

"Oh," she said, kicking at some leaves that had gathered on the roof of the treehouse. "I mean, I'm still a little sad. But I'm also happy." She tossed the ball to Jax, and he caught it without thinking.

He took one hand off the ball and scratched his head, nodding slowly. "Oh, I see." It was clear he didn't.

"You haven't had a lot of girls around here, huh?" She motioned for him to toss the ball back, but he dropped it as he shook his head. "Don't you ever feel a lot of emotions at once?" she asked.

"I guess sometimes I feel . . . happy to be in Neverland but also . . . also . . ."

Man, getting boys to talk about their emotions was hard in any world. "You said sometimes you're sad Peter left?"

He nodded.

"But you also said he wasn't always the best leader, that he was bossy and didn't always listen?"

Jax nodded slowly, like he was still afraid to admit any faults about their beloved Pan.

"So you can still miss him and care about him even though he sometimes made you mad and didn't always listen to what you wanted."

His eyes widened.

"And I bet sometimes you're happy it's your turn to be leader, even though you wish he could come back and be leader again?"

His mouth dropped open. "Yeah! Yeah, that's true!"

She shook her head. *Boys.* "Well, I just realized I'm not sick anymore and I'm really happy about that."

Jax was catching on to the game and urged her toward her next thought. "But . . ."

"But I still miss my mom and wish I could share my happiness with her." She walked to the edge of the roof where a rope was hanging from some of the branches above while she waited for Jax to process what she was saying.

"Now that you're all better, are you going to go home to her?"

Her stomach clenched at the word "home," and she grabbed the rope, trying to stay distracted. "I don't think I can, Jax. I think Neverland is making me better."

"But you'll see your mom and you won't be sad."

"Right, but . . ."

"But you'll be sick."

"Right." This was what her mom wanted. For her to be healthy, to live—to not give up. She couldn't go home now.

"But sometimes sick can be made better," Jax said.

"It's not that kind of sick," she whispered.

"So if you go back you . . ." Jax trailed off and Angela didn't fill in the blank. They both knew what he wasn't saying.

After a pause filled with much dirt kicking and staring at the ground, Jax spoke up again. "Lady Pan?"

"Yes?"

"What about your dad?"

Angela cringed. "What about him?"

"Don't you miss him too?"

Angela swallowed. She was so used to it just being her

and her mom that she forgot other people had dads, and that it was normal to miss both parents when you were away from home. "I don't have a dad."

Jax lifted his eyebrows. "Everyone has a dad."

She wondered when Jax had come to Neverland. It must have been a long time ago, back when most kids had both their moms and their dads instead of being shuffled between houses every other weekend like a lot of the kids at her school.

"Well, I suppose I *have* one. But he left before I was born. It's always been just me and my mom against the world, and honestly, if he didn't care enough about me to even hang around until I was born, I wouldn't have it any other way. Do you miss your dad?"

Jax shook his head. "I don't really remember my dad. But I miss, or at least I think I miss, *having* a dad."

Angela shrugged. "Well, I guess you can't miss what you've never had."

Jax looked up at her, his eyes wide, like he was afraid she'd start crying again. "No wonder you're feeling a lot of things," he said, continuing the cleaning of the leaves she'd started. "Well, there's a little bit of good news," he added, still watching his feet.

"What's that?"

He looked up, his green eyes dancing. "You can stay with us and have adventures forever!"

"Forever," she whispered around a lump in her throat. It seemed like such a long time. But Jax looked so happy and so expectant that she smiled and nodded. "You're right. That is good news. Now tell me, what the heck is this rope for?"

Jax grinned. "It's so we can fly."

"Fly? But . . ."

"Only Peter could fly. It only takes two things, happy thoughts and—"

"Fairy dust," Angela whispered, picturing the now empty bag her mother had poured over her just before she'd left home.

Jax nodded. "But Peter was the only one the fairies liked enough to give fairy dust. So"— he pointed to the rope—"this is how we fly. Want me to show you?"

Angela nodded.

Jax showed her the best spot in the tree to stand and helped secure her foot at the knot in the rope.

He stepped back. "Now just jump, and fly."

He made it sound so simple. "Does anyone ever fall?" she asked, gripping the rope so hard she was afraid it would cut her hands. She'd never been much of a daredevil, preferring her books over the bike stunts, bridge-jumping, and cannonballs of the kids her age.

"Trust Neverland," Jax whispered with reverence.

She took her eyes off the rope and looked toward Jax, his seriousness startling her.

When her gaze met his though, the hard line of his mouth melted into a smile, and he opened his arms like he wanted to embrace the air around him. "She never lets us fall."

It was an odd concept, trusting a place, but as Angela stood in the tree, studying Jax, a soft breeze kissing her cheeks, it made sense. She adjusted her grip on the rope and took one last look at Jax, who was now standing with one hand on a hip and one tucked into the pocket of his pants. His red hair glowed under the midday suns and gave the impression his head was on fire. Angela was convinced that if he moved, the leaves hanging over his head would catch fire, followed by the tree she was standing in, and then the treehouse and then the whole of Neverland would be consumed by the flames started by this boy's hair, and she wondered if that's how he became their leader—that fire that seemed to always be burning within him.

Jax's flame and his fiery passion for Neverland were her last thoughts before she let out a crow and stepped off the tree, trusting Neverland, and the rope she was gripping, to support her as she soared.

And support her it did. There was a moment when her feet left the safety of the tree and gravity took over that she was sure she was going to face plant into the ground. She'd come all the way to Neverland to survive, and now she'd just killed herself by jumping out of a tree. Her mom was going to kill her. And then, as the ground rushed toward her, a breeze kissed her face, sliding around her body like a hug and pushed against her back, driving her not toward the ground but up and away, toward the branches of the trees reaching down from above. She yelped in delight as she felt the subtle push and knew Jax was right. Neverland wouldn't let her fall.

A few hours later every Lost Boy in Neverland was gathered on top of the treehouse roof, and she found herself hoping that Jax's claim about Neverland never letting them fall was true. During her initial try on the rope swing, she'd soared past almost every room in the treehouse, crowing and laughing wildly past Lost Boys playing, sleeping, and lounging lazily. Roused from their tasks by her crazed flight, they'd climbed to the top of the house to watch their newest addition perform this brave feat of daring over and over. And then, of course, they'd each had to prove they were just as brave.

After everyone took a few turns, even Pidge who needed a little extra persuading, the boys stayed gathered on the roof, alternating swinging from the rope and just hanging out in the sun. From this vantage point, Angela could look out across the trees and hills and into the vast expanse of water where the pirate ship had settled a ways offshore after it was driven from the lagoon.

Angela stood on the edge of the roof, her hands on her hips, and studied the ship and its position in the water. Something was bothering her.

"Jax!" she called. "Hey, Jax?" The boy appeared beside her and she pointed to the ship. "Do you notice anything strange about that?"

"The ship? It's out to sea. Exactly where it's supposed to be."

"But doesn't it seem . . . closer than it was yesterday?"

Jax narrowed his eyes and stepped closer to the edge of the roof, and she had to fight an urge to grab the back of his shirt to keep him from plummeting to the earth below.

"The sails," he muttered as he studied the ship, and Angela realized why she was so bothered. Not only did the ship seem closer, but its sails were once again raised, when only yesterday they had lowered them as they'd anchored out at sea.

He looked at her. "The pirates are coming back to Neverland."

"What!?" Pidge peeped, appearing at her side on stealthy feet. "The pirates are back?"

"No," she said. "They're not."

"They're coming back," Jax said.

"We don't *know* that," she said, trying not to scare Pidge, who was jumping nervously from one foot to the other.

"You're the one that pointed it out!" Jax said, not catching on. "The sails are up and it's closer than it was yesterday. They're coming to shore."

"Fine! Yes, that's what it looks like. But we don't know what they're up to. We need to think. We need a carefully thought-out str—"

"Stakeout!" Jax yelled, and the other boys, who hadn't been paying attention, turned and cheered, even though they had no idea what he was talking about.

"It's time to spy on the pirates, boys! Let's—"

"Hey!" Her voice rose over Jax's, and he and the other boys jumped. "I was talking! I know you're the leader here, but you can't just interrupt me like that! That's not how this works."

Jax looked down, and she felt a little bad for scolding; she felt a little like her mother.

"Jax, a stakeout is a good idea, but I don't think we should all go. The smaller the group, the better, agreed?"

"Agreed," he said, reinvigorated by the acceptance of his idea. "Who wants to go?" Every hand went up, and he looked at her and shrugged.

She rolled her eyes. "Who wants to hike for hours and then just sit and *watch* the pirates. There will be no fighting!

Just watching." Almost all the hands lowered. Pidge, who was still at her side, said he would go if she was going, and Tank stepped forward to join the expedition.

"OK," she said. "That should do it. Are we ready to go, Jax?"

Jax nodded and gave the order, "Move out, boys!"

***

Their march ended at the shoreline, which they reached at about the same time as the ship. All the while they'd been moving from their inland hideout, the ship had been making its way steadily toward shore. They didn't watch the lagoon. If the pirates were trying to be stealthy, they wouldn't risk coming to shore there. And they didn't. Angela and the boys climbed one of the highest trees so they could get a sense of what was happening on the ship.

"They're not dropping anchor," Jax said, pointing to the spot reserved for that. There was no one there. "They're not even steering."

They all looked at the helm of the ship and saw Jax was right. A man stood behind the wheel of the ship, but he held a half-empty bottle of rum and was swaying back and forth with the rhythm of the ship and shouting something they could not hear. He wasn't even touching the wheel. They looked around the ship and found the other pirates in a similar state; waving rum bottles heartily, swaying back and forth or falling down and laughing. They were all drunk. It appeared their trip to shore had been nothing more than a drunken accident.

Angela looked at Jax, and he shrugged, apparently satisfied there was no immediate threat. But before she could lift a hand and motion for Pidge and Tank to start their descent from the tree, a movement on the ship made her pause.

"Look," she said, pointing to a porthole near the end of the ship closest to shore. A rope that reached all the way down to the water had just appeared, followed by the head of a man. The man checked the area around the ship, glanced up toward the party on deck, and then behind him, and when he seemed satisfied no one was watching, he pulled himself through the porthole, gripped the rope, and began to lower himself down the side of the ship.

"What's he doing?" Jax asked

"He's gotta come to shore," Angela said. "It's his only option."

"What if he's a spy for Smee?" Tank said. The kid didn't say much, but when he did, he made good points.

"We can't let him wander around the island," she said, and all the boys nodded.

The man had reached the water and was swimming toward shore. Eager to beat him there, they all quickly descended the tree.

When they reached the ground and started toward the beach, Jax came up beside her. "He might be here for you, ya know."

"What do you mean?"

"Smee isn't always a dummy. He has his moments and he might have figured out who you are and sent someone to . . . well, you know." He raked his finger across his throat and crossed his eyes.

Subtle, she thought.

"You should stay behind us when we get there."

She snorted. "No way." But Jax did have a point—he could be after her and she was completely unprotected. She looked behind her at Pidge, who looked terrified at the idea of confronting this pirate. "Pidge, you stay behind us and give me your knife." Everyone had some sort of weapon, even if they never used them. Pidge's weapon was befitting of his size. He gladly handed over the small knife, the blade barely the length of her hand, that he kept tucked in the back of his pants. She looked back at Jax. "I can protect myself, thank you very much."

They reached the beach just moments before the man, and as though they'd all discussed it, Jax, Tank, and Angela formed a line at the edge of the water where he would come ashore, Pidge just behind them, ready to crow for help if they needed it.

The man wasn't looking up when he reached the point in the water shallow enough to stand. His swim had exhausted him and his head was hanging down, his wet hair forming a curtain around his face, his drab, dark clothes clinging to him.

When he looked up, he jumped. The three of them stood, weapons extended, forming a small, probably not very intimidating, blockade between him and the beach. If he wanted to go any farther, he would have to go through them . . . which he probably could have, easily, but since they were in Neverland, they pretended.

"Welcome to Neverland, pirate," Angela said, pretending

to be someone who was used to confronting pirates. "State your business before we slice you."

To everyone's surprise, instead of reaching for a weapon, the man lifted his arms to the sky. "I mean no harm."

Jax scoffed.

"I swear, I don't want to hurt anyone. Here." He reached slowly down toward his side, and Jax and Angela both raised their weapons higher, though Jax's sword was slightly more intimidating than her butter knife. He pulled his sword out of its sheath and quickly flipped it so its handle was extended forward. He lifted his gaze and his dark eyes met Angela's as he motioned not to Jax, who was known to the pirates as the leader of the Lost Boys, but to her. "Here," he said, "take it."

She reached out and her hand closed around the handle of the sword. Her fingers slid easily into the grooves he'd made in the hilt over years of use. "Who are you? Why are you here?" she said a little less aggressively, keeping the sword and the knife on him.

"My name is Lamont, and I came to find you . . . Angela."

CHAPTER 6

She was confident and fierce, and her brown eyes studied him like her mother's once had. At this first glimpse of his fearless daughter, Lamont wanted nothing more than to take away her worry and any fear she might be hiding. To take care of her as he should have done thirteen years ago. But she was not ready to be cared for. She was standing just a few steps ahead of the Lost Boys, a fact they either didn't notice or didn't bother trying to change. The arm holding his sword was steady, steadier than he would expect for someone he assumed had never used a weapon or faced any sort of foe, and aimed directly at him. Her other arm was placed protectively in front of the smallest boy standing to her left. Her cheeks were pink, and flushed with adrenaline, and the suns had brought out a line of freckles across her nose and cheeks. Lamont smiled in spite of himself. She'd been in Neverland only a short time, but it suited her.

There was a long silence following his announcement, only broken when the boy next to her whispered, "Who's Angela?"

Angela rolled her eyes and Lamont almost laughed. Without looking away from her, he said, "*This* is Angela. Angela Margaret Jackson. Daughter of Moira Jackson. Great-granddaughter of your Peter Pan."

"Oh . . . yeah," the boy said.

The descendant who wouldn't exist if Smee's plan had gone the way he wanted. If Lamont had followed orders.

"You mean," Smee had snarled when Lamont had revealed his identity, "you were supposed to kill Pan's descendants and instead you created *more*? Do you have a death wish, pirate?"

Lamont had stayed silent. If he wanted to get Angela safely out of Neverland, he knew he needed to tread carefully with Smee.

"Why shouldn't I kill you where you stand?"

"You want the girl gone?"

"Of course."

"Do you have a plan?"

"We're pirates. We'll kill her and any Lost Boy that stands in our way."

But Lamont couldn't have that so he'd proposed a second option.

"How do you know who I am?" Angela said, stepping closer to him, the weapons in her hands still outstretched.

"I knew who you were the moment Neverland woke up. And I knew how much I loved you the moment your mother told me she was pregnant."

A cool breeze picked up off the ocean and swept across the beach as Angela's eyes flashed with understanding.

"Uh-oh," the boy whispered from behind her, and Lamont realized why he was worried. Angela's knuckles went white as her grip on his weapon tightened and the wind suddenly picked up around them. Her mouth opened and closed with what he imagined were years of unanswered questions, but none came out as the gentle breeze coming in off the water gained strength and picked up sand and leaves and branches. It began to swirl around them until they were at the center of a small cyclone of debris, sea mist, anger, and hurt.

"What's happening?" one of the boys yelled.

Lamont didn't move as the boy next to Angela answered over the wind, "It's her! Neverland will always be connected to a Pan. It's reacting to her!"

"Angela!" Lamont called above the wind, trying to offer some sort of condolence or explanation. "Please, calm down and—" It was the wrong thing to say.

"Calm down!? Are you *really* going to tell me to calm down right now? You *abandoned* us before I was even born

. . . You left and you never called, never wrote, never visited . . . You never even *saw* me!"

Lamont flinched at her words and he stepped forward hoping to clear the air. "Left you? Angela, I—"

"Now you're standing in front of me, in *Neverland*, as a *pirate*, and you want me to *calm down*?" On these last words, the small vortex spinning around them expanded, and from out over the water, dark clouds appeared on the horizon.

"Lady Pan, please." The boy came up next to her and timidly put his hand on her shoulder. "You're upsetting Neverland. Remember, it's tied to you. Don't do it for him, do it for us. Don't let Neverland go dark again. We need you to bring it back."

Lamont watched as her grip on the weapons she was holding loosened, and the boy's words seemed to break through the wall of anger she'd started building. She studied Lamont as she took a deep breath, and the sand and branches and leaves began to fall around them. She turned to the boy whose hand was on her shoulder. "Thank you, Jax."

The boy named Jax nodded and stepped back.

Lamont was still standing in about a foot of water, shaking from the cold, as her brown eyes moved to his. He hoped that the calming weather meant she was feeling a little more welcoming and that he could explain himself, but that wasn't the case.

Without a word she turned away from him and walked up the beach, calling over her shoulder, "We're leaving, boys."

"But what about him?" Jax called.

"We have his weapon."

"We can't just let him wander around Neverland. That's what *you* said and you're right. He could find our hideouts and report back to the pirates."

"That's not why I'm—"

"Quiet, pirate," Jax snapped and turned back to Angela. "It's bad enough you're . . ."

Angela whipped around to face Jax. "I'm *what?*"

"Well," Jax looked from Angela to Lamont and back again. "He's a . . . so you're a . . ."

"Are you seriously worried because I'm half pirate?"

Jax froze, and Lamont had to stop himself from laughing at the ridiculousness of the situation. Three completely lost Lost Boys who had no idea how to deal with the situation in front of them, one overwhelmed teenage girl, and one sopping wet, shivering pirate.

Lamont took a slow step forward. "Jax, is it?"

Jax jumped back and lifted his sword.

"It's OK. You don't need to worry about Angela. I might be a pirate, but her mother . . . her mother was all Pan. She was loyal and kind and strong—everything I've failed to be in my life."

He was talking faster, growing desperate. He had to stay with Angela, and he could see that meant gaining the trust of the boys. He'd made two promises, one to himself and one to his captain. He only intended to keep one of them, but he needed time—time to get them to accept him.

"Your men are not ready to fight Lost Boys," he'd told Smee. "You've been enjoying a quiet Neverland, why spoil it with a fight? If I can get her to trust me, I can convince her to go home, back to her mother . . . away from Neverland. You'll go back to your quiet life without ever having lifted your sword."

Smee's eyes narrowed and danced between his men and Lamont. He stepped closer to Lamont and in a low voice said, "This girl insulted me, Lamont. She embarrassed me in front of my men. You get her out of Neverland, or I will."

"Yes, sir."

"Well," Smee had shouted and grinned, "let's get this scallywag to shore! He's got a job to do!"

Lamont shook his head to clear away Smee's voice and brought his focus back to Jax. "You know you can trust her or you wouldn't be here now, together."

"She saved my life, Jax!" a small Lost Boy squeaked. "She's no pirate and you know it!"

"Fine! She's not. But *he* is!"

"I didn't come here to cause trouble." He tried to keep his voice steady. Begging wouldn't go over well with the Lost Boys. "I came here to find Angela. And I have. I just wanted to see you. I have no other business on the island."

Jax snorted. "Like we would take a pirate's word for truth."

"Never trust a pirate," Angela muttered.

Lamont cocked his head, studying her, and then continued. "You don't understand. I . . . ." He sighed. "It's a really long story."

"Story?" The small boy who had defended Angela spoke up. "We love stories!"

"Pidge . . ." But Angela's warning was ignored. The boy was already sitting in the sand, cross-legged and at attention.

Jax looked down at him, then back up at Angela, and shrugged. "Maybe it will help." He turned to Lamont. "Yes, pirate. Tell us a story. And make it a good one."

As three boys sat cross-legged in front of him and his daughter stood with her arms crossed over her chest, pretending she wasn't paying attention, Lamont began his tale.

***

Lamont was never sure why Smee chose him for the mission to destroy Pan's family. He'd never been much of a pirate, preferring his own solitude to the company of the loud and raucous crew, the books they pillaged over the rum and gold. Whatever Smee's reasoning, one dark and gloomy day, he pulled Lamont aside and voiced his fears: that a descendant of Pan who still believed in Neverland would come back and destroy the quiet calm Smee had grown to love. He knew Pan's kids never came back to Neverland after their rescue, and that probably meant they'd stopped believing, but he didn't know how many more generations there were in the Pan line . . . and how many still believed. All it would take was one Pan to bring Neverland back to life, and Smee did not want that. So he gave Lamont a mission.

He was to leave Neverland, locate Pan's family, find out if any living relatives still believed, and take care of them. Thrilled with the idea of getting off the ship for a little while, Lamont had accepted.

Once he got to the other world, it didn't take him long to

find his target. He knew where the family had been living, so he asked around. They were a nice family, people said, quiet and normal and respectable . . . except for one of them. One of them went into the city as soon as she was able and was trying to make a living writing about Peter Pan. She read her stories all over town, sent them off to publishers, published them herself—anything she could to get her tales out there. But, they said, no one cared about those types of stories anymore. They were silly and childish and not what kids today wanted to read. So, she worked in a bar in the city to make ends meet.

He found her there, serving drinks and laughing like she had fairy dust in her eyes, and from the very first moment he saw Peter Pan's granddaughter, he knew he would fail his mission. As a pirate, he'd seen a lot of women, but he'd never seen one like Moira. She moved so naturally behind the bar, almost like she was flying. And her cheeks were red, as though she'd been out in the cool evening. And her laugh. Oh, her laugh was like a waterfall. It washed over Lamont and made him shiver and refreshed him all at the same time. It was obvious, at least to him, that she believed in other worlds and magic, and all the things she wrote about. It was written all over her face and in the way she smiled and in the way her eyes danced. Her other customers just thought she was friendly, sort of special, and a little different, but he knew there was Neverland in her blood.

He sat down in front of her, trying to look normal, like he was a part of her world, but she immediately knew he wasn't. She didn't know who he was, of course, but she knew he wasn't like the other inhabitants of her bar stools. She leaned on the bar to ask him for his order, and her eyes narrowed at his ponytail and tattoos. He could tell she sensed something in him, but she was too polite to say anything.

"What'll it be, mate?" she'd asked.

Mo was a firecracker, and from the moment that first spark snapped between them, they were inseparable. She said she didn't care that he was just passing through or that he had to leave once he did what he came into town to do.

"Well, whatever it is, get it done and we'll leave together," she said. "We could go to New York! I could pitch my books to some real publishers, not the slop buckets around here."

She said she didn't care about his past and scoffed when he told her she wouldn't love him if she knew who he really was.

"I know who you are right now, in this moment . . . and that's all that matters—these moments we have right in front of us are the moments that make our hearts."

"Make our hearts what?" he asked.

"Make them what they are."

With every moment that passed, Lamont fell deeper and deeper in love with her . . . and every moment that passed brought him closer to a moment of truth. What would happen if he didn't do what he came to do? Could he leave behind his life as a pirate and stay with Mo forever? Could they truly start a new life together?

A pirate's loyalty to his crew runs deep, and he had been a crew member on the *Jolly Roger* for as long as he could remember, but sometimes new loyalties arise and priorities change. Sometimes, something comes along that is bigger than you are and you know exactly where you're meant to be.

When Mo told him she was pregnant, that's what happened.

He didn't care about his crew or his old life as a pirate. He didn't care about Smee's orders or even Neverland. He cared about Mo and the child they would have together.

The day after she told him the news, he went to a pawn shop. He used the sword he'd carried for as long as he'd been a pirate to trade for a small diamond ring—much smaller than he would have liked, but he knew Mo wouldn't care. He left his sword with a very curious pawnbroker and stepped out onto the street, ready to pledge his love to Moira and dedicate his life to taking care of her and their child.

***

"But what happened?"

"Why didn't you stay?"

Lamont had trailed off, leaving the story hanging in the already heavy air around them. He couldn't do it, he couldn't go on. He could hear Mo chatting happily about naming the baby after the great Wendy, already sure the baby would be a girl.

"Wendy Moira *Angela* Darling. She'll grow up knowing all about Wendy and Peter and their adventures. I'll tell her everything there is to know about her heritage, and she will grow up believing. Not like the rest of my ungrateful family. And I'll tell you and you can help me tell her . . ."

That was when everything started to break.

When he didn't answer, Angela looked up from the sand where she'd finally sat down.

The boys were enthralled, their necks craned as they leaned toward Lamont to capture every word of his story, the story of their Pan's family, the continuation of his legacy. But Angela wasn't sold. It was clear she thought she knew how this story ended, and he couldn't bring himself to tell her the truth, yet. He couldn't tell her about the look in her mother's eyes when she'd learned the truth or the cold flatness of her voice when she'd said, "Just go."

"What is it?" the little one named Pidge said. "What's next?"

Lamont sighed and Angela lifted her eyebrows, inviting an answer she would find convincing enough to forgive him, but Lamont bowed his head.

"I changed my mind. I went back to the pawnshop. Got my sword back and returned to my life as a pirate.

"When I got back to the ship, I sought out Smee. I knew what I had to tell him and I could only hope he would believe me. I found him in his favorite spot doing his favorite thing, drinking rum, already three sheets to the wind, which was lucky for me.

"'Ahh . . . La–mo–tent,' he slurred when he saw me. 'You're back. Do you bring me news?'

"'I do, sir. It's good news.'

"'Oh, good! I do so love good news. It's always so . . . so . . . good!' He stood up and threw an arm around my shoulder, his breath and body odor erasing all traces of lavender left on my clothes or hair. 'Do tell . . .'"

The boys all giggled at his impersonation of an intoxicated

Smee, but Angela was stone-faced.

"'There's no one left, sir. No one in his family believes in Pan or Neverland.'

"'Oh, that's wonderful news!' He removed his arm and stumbled over to his supply of rum, grabbing another bottle and handing it to me. 'Let's drink, Lommy! Drink to the end of Pan's reign in Neverland!'"

"Lommy!" the boys howled and Lamont continued.

"I didn't want to drink to the sentiment, but I desperately wanted to drink away the icy block of sadness sitting in the middle of my chest. I raised my bottle when Smee did and threw back a swig. By the time I pulled the bottle from my lips, Smee was passed out on the floor and my family was safe."

The boys were still recovering from hearing about a drunk Smee, and Jax wiped away a gleeful tear and looked up. "But wait . . . *why*? Why did you leave?"

"It doesn't matter," Angela said before Lamont could answer, and the boys all turned to her. "It doesn't matter *why* he left, he still left. And he can't change that."

Jax, Pidge, and Tank all winced at her words. Lamont knew Lost Boys were used to hearing stories with happy endings, and this story didn't have one.

"You're right," he said. "I can't."

Jax stood up and looked between the two of them. "Well, what now?"

"Now, *we* go back to the hideout," Angela said.

She motioned to the boys and they nodded. He wasn't in yet.

"You can't go back to your hideout." He took a step forward, slowly moving out of the water.

Angela lifted the weapons in her hands, reading his response as a threat. "And just why is that?"

"Because we're not alone."

As they were talking, distracted by stories and arguments and talks of loyalty, down the beach a small rowboat had come ashore. Lamont had watched out of the corner of his eye as the pirate hid the boat among bushes and debris along the shore and had started to make his way toward them. Now, he was hidden among the trees behind them, waiting for the right moment to follow them back to the hideout and report to Smee. But Lamont wasn't going to wait.

"We see you, pirate!" he called, and the moment he was revealed, the man let out a grunt and pushed through the foliage, barreling toward the boys and Angela.

Lamont pushed through the small group, moving in front of them, and as he did he realized Angela still had his weapon. Rather than demand she turn it over, Lamont widened his stance, planted his feet in the sand, tucked his neck and head, and crouched. The pirate's momentum worked against him, and Lamont shifted left to avoid his blade, shoving his shoulder into the man's chest and sending him flying into the sand, onto his back. Despite their mistrust, the boys cheered as the pirate hit the ground, and Lamont smiled. There wasn't much he could do from here without a blade, but before he could consider his actions, he heard his name and turned toward Angela.

She twirled Lamont's sword in her hand and tossed it back to him. "That's yours, pirate."

He caught the sword by the handle and swung back

around to face the man now trying to crawl through the sand toward the sword that had gone flying when he did. He knew the boys would be itching to fight, but he had to keep this one to himself. His long legs carried him to the pirate and away from the group in a few easy strides, and he reached down to grab the weapon the man had just started to wrap his fingers around. Lamont pulled it from his grasp, shoved a boot into his back, and called over his shoulder.

"Jax, catch!" He tossed the sword, and Jax caught it with a triumphant crow. "Keep it away from him."

Whether Jax trusted Lamont or not didn't matter at the moment—for the Lost Boys, a weaponless pirate was the best kind, so he moved away from Lamont and his captive as Tank dragged Pidge away from the tussle. Angela stood, studying his every move. Lamont knew what he *should* do with the pirate Smee had sent behind his back to spy on Angela. But if he took this pirate's life in front of his daughter, she'd hate him more than she already did.

With the group a safe distance away, he reached down and flipped the pirate onto his back, pressing his boot into his chest and a blade into his neck. The pirate winced and growled.

"What are you playing at, La—"

But Lamont pressed the blade harder, and he stopped talking.

Loudly, so the boys and Angela could hear him, he told the pirate, "You get off this beach and you take a message back to Smee. Any pirate that steps foot on shore will face me. And I won't be so lenient with the next one, ya understand?"

He stomped down and forced a groan from the pirate's

chest.

Leaning down to grab the collar of his shirt, he whispered into his ear, "We had a plan. You tell Smee I've got this covered, and if he wants the girl gone, he needs to let me work."

Pulling the pirate to his feet, he shoved him back toward his boat and called, "Stay off this island!"

The pirate stumbled through the sand, and Lamont watched the shore, his chest rising and falling, his heart pounding, until the man was back in his boat and pushing off toward the ship. Only then did he relax his grip on the sword in his hand and turn back to the group.

They were all watching him, probably for any signs he was going to turn on them and join his crewmate, but he stayed still. The next move was on them.

Jax broke the silence. "You should have killed him. Your loyalty still lies with the pirates."

Lamont spoke slowly, "Smee sent him to find your hide-out. If I had killed him, the whole crew would have come ashore, ready to hunt you lot down and kill you. Is that what you want?"

The boys started to cheer, and Jax raised the pirate's sword with a "Yea—" but Angela cut him off.

"No. He's right. It was the right call."

The boys went quiet again and Lamont nodded toward his daughter, a silent thank-you for her approval. But she was still eyeing the sword in his hand cautiously, the one she'd willingly returned to him.

"Here." He swung the blade so the handle was facing her. "I don't need a weapon." He tossed her the sword and she caught it easily. "You handle it well."

"Well, I guess it's in my blood," she said flatly. She handed Pidge back his knife and lowered the sword to her side as she turned to march back up the beach. "Let's go, boys."

"But what about him?" Jax said.

Angela stopped walking. "If he's not running back to the pirates, we better keep an eye on him." She glanced behind her, toward the boys. "New game, don't let the pirate out of your sight."

Chapter 7

Keeping an eye on her pirate father was not a problem. All he wanted to do was follow them around the island like a little lost puppy. Angela ignored him as they made their way back to the treehouse, but it didn't take long before the curiosity of the boys got the better of them. They'd seen he could be trusted and now they were interested. She couldn't blame them. It had probably been a very long time since they'd been around a man who wasn't trying to maim or kill them, and she knew how much they missed Peter.

Tank and Pidge bombarded him with questions while Jax stayed quiet and walked with her, sharing her silence and cautious skepticism of this new development.

"How did you become a pirate?"

"How many men have you killed?"

"What's Smee like?"

"What do you *do* all day?"

"Why do you try so hard to kill us?"

"Why are you so bad at it?"

Lamont laughed. "Well," he asked, directing his response at Tank, "how did you become a Lost Boy?"

Tank stopped walking and his eyes widened. "I . . . I don't really remember." He looked panicked for a moment, like he'd forgotten an important answer on a test, but Lamont just smiled and nodded.

"Neverland does that to you . . . it makes you forget. You've all been here a long time. It's not surprising that you've forgotten your old life."

"I haven't forgotten," Angela said, still walking. "I remember my mother and how hard it was for her to raise me by herself and how hard she worked to share her Peter Pan stories with the world and how sometimes she worked two jobs and still found time to write at night and pitch her stories. I remember how proud she was when they got picked up and how surprised she was when they got popular because she never knew how good she was no matter how many times I told her. I remember that her laugh was contagious and she always smelled like . . ." She stopped walking. "She always smelled like . . . like . . ." Angela could see her mom's face in front of her. She could hear her laugh echoing through their house as she watched her favorite show, but Angela couldn't catch the scent that always drifted behind her as she walked or that lingered on Angela's clothes after she hugged her.

It was a smell that had been there for as long as she could remember and probably even before. By the time Angela became aware of it, it was already familiar, and it was only when she reached middle school that she realized it was something her mom applied every morning and not just the way she smelled. And now she couldn't remember what it was called or even smell it in her memories.

"Oh no," she gasped, leaning forward and resting a hand against a nearby tree. "I don't remember. It's gone. She's fading. It's already happening . . . I can't . . ."

As the ground was coming up to meet her, she felt a hand on her shoulder, and before her knees buckled, the steadiness of the weight on her shoulder started to even things out.

A deep voice from behind her mumbled, "Lavender. She always smelled like lavender."

Angela breathed deep and leaned her head back to stop the tears that had begun pooling in her eyes from falling down her cheeks and whispered, "Lavender. That's right. It was in a small glass bottle . . ."

"A bottle that her best friend sent her every year at Christmas . . ."

"Because she'd grown up on a lavender farm, and Mom used to love playing there in the summers. She said the smell reminded her of . . ." She looked around her at the trees of Neverland and at the confused faces of her Lost Boy friends. "Of never growing up."

Lamont was nodding, his hand still on her shoulder. "That's right. You see? You're not forgetting her. You could never forget her. Just like I haven't."

"But why haven't you?"

Lamont shrugged. "Why do the boys all remember Peter? And Wendy? I think Neverland lets us keep what we want to keep. If you want to remember her, you will."

Angela offered a half-hearted smile, grateful for his help but not reassured by his words. Her hands were still shaking as she straightened up and kept walking, thinking about what might happen to her the longer she was in Neverland. If she was already forgetting the little things, how long would it be before she, like the boys, forgot her old life completely? Even if she wanted to remember, Neverland or not, memories always faded with time.

***

Night was falling when they reached the hideout. A hammock hung just outside the entrance to the treehouse, and Angela pointed, indicating that's where Lamont could sleep.

After designating a watch schedule to keep an eye on the pirate throughout the night, Angela and the boys climbed inside. They each peeled off when they reached their claimed rooms, but she kept climbing all the way to the roof. When she arrived, she went to the edge and sat down, letting her legs dangle over the side.

From behind her, there was a squeak and a strangled, "Be

careful!"

She jumped and turned to find Pidge holding his arms out like he was going to grab her if she fell. "Pidge, you scared me! Don't do that to a person sitting on a ledge."

"I'm sorry."

She smiled and waved him over. "It's OK. It's safe as long as you're careful. Come sit by me."

Reluctantly, Pidge inched across the roof and slowly sat down, keeping his legs tucked under him. She didn't know how such a fearful, dainty soul ever became a Lost Boy, but she was glad he was here.

"See?" she said. "It's nice, huh?"

He nodded. "It's beautiful."

The suns were hanging just at the horizon, but the giant Neverland moons, that looked so much like her moon it made her homesick, were already in the sky, hanging out next to the suns like they were trying to fill each other in on the events of their days before switching shifts.

"Lady Pan?"

"Yes, Pidge?"

"You're not sick anymore, right?"

"No, I don't think I am."

"That's good."

She looked down at his small, sharp features. "Do you know about sickness?" Most of the Lost Boys seemed to not believe in such things, though as she'd learned from Jax, it was often one big game of pretend.

Pidge nodded. "It's why I came to Neverland."

"You remember coming to Neverland?" she asked. If someone who had been here as long as Pidge still remembered his life, maybe she wouldn't forget hers.

"Some days, yes. Some days, no. You help me remember because you remind me of my mother."

"I do? Why?"

"She was sick too."

Angela swallowed. "That's why you came to Neverland? Your mother was sick?"

"I came to Neverland because I was scared."

Angela wondered if that's how everyone ended up in Neverland—the fear of facing something that was too big to handle.

"She got so sick that I wasn't allowed to be in the room with her. All I wanted to do was take care of her, but I wasn't allowed. But it didn't matter because even when I was allowed to see her . . . she wasn't my mother."

Angela thought about how she would feel if the roles of her illness had been reversed, if she'd had to watch her mom go through the same things she'd gone through over the last few years. During the worst of her illness, sometimes Angela looked in the mirror and no longer recognized herself. But what if she'd looked at her mom and no longer recognized the biggest source of comfort and love in her life? She thought about Pidge searching his mother's face for some sign that she was still there . . . and finding none.

"Oh, Pidge . . ." Her voice was a shaky whisper.

"That's why I gave that name when I came here. She told me that when I was born, my lips were so pointy they looked like a beak. And then when I was little, I liked chasing the pigeons that gathered outside of our apartment. When she was sick, I missed her even though she was still there. I started to think about my life when she was really gone, and it just seemed so...so empty. So, I ran away. I just ran out of the house one day and everyone was so busy taking care of her that no one noticed. I made it all the way to the park on the other side of town before I stopped running. That's where I was when Peter found me and brought me here."

"And your mom? What happened to her?"

"I don't know. I've never been back. I guess she died. That's what happens there, right? People die?"

She nodded and swallowed around the lump in her throat, not wanting to spoil the beautiful evening with a rain shower. "Yes, that's what happens."

Pidge lifted his chin as though that settled everything. "Then you're better off here." He stood up and brushed off his hands on his pants, as though washing them of his previous life. "I don't want you to die too."

She had to clear her throat to speak. "I know, Pidge," she whispered.

"Good night, Lady Pan."

Pidge turned and walked to the center of the roof, but before he could climb down the chute, she stopped him. "Pidge?"

He turned. "Yes?"

"Do you think you'll ever go back?"

Without hesitation, he shook his head. "There's nothing for me there. All the people I ever loved are gone."

Angela nodded and Pidge smiled again, turning back to the ladder and climbing down into the chute that would take him to the lower levels.

Angela knew she should make her way down to her bed,

but for a moment she couldn't move. Her mind was filled with thoughts of her mom, her home, and Pidge's statement, "All the people I ever loved are gone." She knew what would happen if she returned, but almost more scary than that was what would happen if she stayed.

***

As soon as Angela stepped out of the treehouse into the early morning breeze, Lamont was there, waiting.

"Good morning, Angela."

"Mmm . . . " she replied, pushing past him. If she had to pick the one thing from her old life she missed the most, it was caffeine.

"I know you're angry with me, but you're my daughter and I'd love to know more about you."

She also missed peaceful mornings with her mom, drinking tea silently until they were both coherent enough to have a conversation.

"How did you end up in Neverland?" he pressed.

She ignored him and kept walking. He followed.

"Is your mom OK?"

"Don't talk about my mom." The mention of her pulled Angela through the fog of sleep. She heard Lamont sigh as she continued to walk in silence. She didn't know where she was going, but in Neverland you didn't have to.

"She really was quite wonderful," Lamont mumbled, so low that Angela nearly missed it. "It must have been really great growing up with a mom like that, huh?"

Angela kept walking.

"I bet she was a great mother. I knew she would be the moment she told me she was pregnant."

Angela shook her head but didn't respond. He'd left. She couldn't believe anything he said about how much he loved her mom or how wonderful he thought she was.

"Talk to me, Angela! Don't you think I deserve to know something?"

That did it. She spun around, her fists balled at her sides—it was probably a good thing she wasn't carrying his sword. He stopped in his tracks and flinched. Her anger coursed through her, energizing her faster than the strongest tea.

"Deserve? *Deserve?* How could you possibly think you deserve anything from me? Because I share your genes? You're not even a name on a birth certificate to me and you think you *deserve* the chance to be all fatherly just because we stumbled across each other in Neverland?" She turned back to the path ahead of her and kept walking, a gust of wind pushing against her back and leaving a trail of swirling leaves in her wake. She thought maybe she'd shocked him into silence, but no such luck.

"You don't know . . ."

She wheeled around again and the trees shifted and bent around them. "What? What don't I know?"

He opened his mouth and then closed it again. "You . . . you don't know how hard it was to leave."

She scoffed and started walking again. "I'm sorry it was so hard on *you.*"

There was a long silence as the wind died down and they

walked through the trees, slapping at bugs.

"How did *you* end up here, anyway?" she said over a small buzzing sound in her ear. She wasn't really sure how to make small talk with a pirate who also happened to be her father . . . not that he even deserved that much.

"Oh, the same way most people end up in Neverland, I guess. Looking for a different life."

"I wasn't looking for a different life," she said, but she was having a hard time concentrating on the conversation as the buzzing sound in her ear grew louder.

"Well, how did you—?"

But she cut him off. "Do you hear that?" she asked, turning around to face him.

He was batting the air around his head absentmindedly but looking at her. "Yea, I guess I do. Is it . . . ?"

Suddenly, there was a streak of black between them. Lamont jumped back and Angela felt a whoosh of air from whatever it had been.

"What the—?" But before he could say anything else, there was another streak behind him, and Angela jumped as a puff of air went over her shoulder and tickled her hair. At first, none of the puffs made contact even as the buzzing grew louder and the number of streaks increased. And then—

"Ow!" Lamont exclaimed, grabbing his ear.

"What . . . Oh!" There was a sharp prick on her chin, but before she could tell him, there was another on her ear and then her arm. "What *are* they?" she asked, hoping his years in Neverland had given him a little more insight into what was happening than she had.

His arms over his head, Lamont peeked out between his forearms. "I have an idea and I really think we should get out of here."

He was right. The frequency of pricks was intensifying, and each one became more painful as they started to hit the same spots over and over. She was waving her arms trying to make contact with whatever was assaulting them, but she met only air.

"Uhh!" she yelled, giving another swipe, and that was when her hand made contact with something. Its progress stopped, it froze in the air for a split second, and she was able to see the body of a woman held in midair by a pair of shiny, translucent wings.

"It's . . . it's . . ."

"It's a fairy!" Lamont yelled, grabbing her elbow and pulling. "We need to get out of here."

"But aren't fairies—" She was about to say "nice" when the one in front of her lifted her hand to reveal a tiny knife no longer than Angela's pinky nail. Knife raised, the pixie resumed her progress through the air . . . toward Angela's face.

"Hey!" She ducked and let Lamont pull her back the direction they'd come.

"Fairies are vicious when they want to be. If you haven't established a relationship with one, you don't want to be anywhere near them. Peter used Tink and her friends against the pirates a few times. It looks like with Pan gone, they don't have any allegiances." He was running with his arms in front of his face, and Angela wasn't far behind.

"But what did we do?" she yelled.

"It doesn't matter. We don't want to hang around to find out."

As they ran back down the trail toward the treehouse, she could hear something behind her, an uneven hum as though hundreds of voices were whispering at the same time.

"They're behind us," she yelled as they approached the treehouse.

Jax was out front, swinging his sword at the empty air in front of him, maybe practicing for his next pirate encounter. When he heard her yelling, he turned and his face fell.

"What did you do?" he called.

"It's fairies," Lamont yelled. "Take cover!"

"You went into fairy territory!?"

They were both breathless when they reached him and Angela leaned forward, bracing her hands on her hips. "Well, I didn't know! Why wouldn't you tell me there were murderous bugs living in the forest surrounding your hide—ow!"

They didn't like being called murderous bugs. She rubbed the back of her neck, completely exposed due to her short hair. "What do we do?" She ducked as another blur whizzed by her ear.

"Mostly we just hide until they wear themselves out," Jax said, putting his hands over his ears.

From beside her, Lamont tried to form a canopy over her head with his arms and a large leaf he'd found on the ground, but she batted him away and ducked out from under it.

While they were talking, the fairies made their way inside the treehouse, and she could hear boy after boy yelping as each realized the fairies had arrived. It sounded like the fairies liked to do more than just poke at people.

"You mean you just let them destroy your home and attack you?" She was bobbing side to side and occasionally ducking as she talked, doing her best to dodge the predatory pixies.

Lamont batted at one near her shoulder and tried to step behind her to form a shield.

"I'm *fine*," she said, moving away from him.

Jax lifted his eyebrows. "Yeah, Lamont. She can take care of herself."

If she hadn't been so annoyed, she would have laughed, but with her skin breaking out in red welts from the incessant pricks and her head aching from the constant buzzing, she was in no mood for a chuckle. She also wasn't in the mood to run and hide or let these males take their time coming up with a better plan.

She rolled her eyes and, with a disgusted groan, pushed Jax out of the way and entered the treehouse. She climbed past the sound of clattering swords and squeaking Lost Boys and found the ladder leading to the roof. She pulled herself up until she reached the top and jumped up.

"Freaking fairies?" she mumbled as she crossed the roof, stomping across the boards below her, her voice rising as she did. "Seriously, Neverland? Give me a break!"

First, the loitering pirates, then the snooty mermaids, then her flippin' dad shows up, and now fairies with 'tude? She'd had enough. Where the heck was her bug spray?

Bug spray. That was it. Obviously, she didn't have any and she didn't think it would do anything to them if she did, but *they* didn't know that.

"Angela!" Her dad's head appeared through the opening in the roof as she made her way to the rope swing. "What are you doing?" He was breathing hard from trying to keep up with her.

"Getting rid of the fairies," she said, gripping the rope.

She looked back at Lamont and, with a grin at the shock and worry lining his face, stepped one foot off the edge of the roof and jumped.

The air was thick with the psycho bugs, and she closed her eyes to keep them from getting poked out. She could hear tiny squeals of surprise as she pushed through a cloud of them, knocking a few off course.

"You fairies better scram," she yelled. "These Lost Boys might let you wreak havoc on their lives, but I'm here now!"

She swung back and forth through the air as she yelled, her voice carrying into the treehouse and beyond. "I come from the other world, and I bring weapons the Lost Boys know nothing about!" She gripped the rope with one hand and dug her feet in as she quickly reached around and grabbed the inhaler she'd started carrying with her when she got sick, the inhaler she hadn't needed since coming to Neverland. "This spray will take you lot out faster than a choir singing about not believing in fairies in an endless encore!" The buzzing intensified as a few saw the canister and began spreading the word back through the crowd. "If you don't make yourself scarce, I'll start spraying!"

***

She could actually hear herself think as she landed back on the roof, the buzzing cloud now back in the woods where it belonged. Jax had joined Lamont. His red hair was even more disheveled than usual, and his green eyes were wide.

"Do you really have bug spray?" he asked.

"Of course not," she said, tossing him the useless inhaler.

"Tricky, tricky," he muttered, staring down at it.

She shrugged and started toward the ladder. She was ready for a nap.

"You really can take care of yourself, huh?" Lamont said.

"It's what I was taught," she replied as she moved toward the chute.

Jax was still shaking his head at the inhaler. "Would have been nice to have this when we had to clear them out of this part of the woods."

Angela stopped walking. "You *what?*"

"Well, when Peter stopped coming back, we wanted a new treehouse in a new section of the forest. A new start, ya know? This was the biggest clearing, but it was overrun with fairies and their little houses."

"Jax, you didn't." Her stomach clenched. It was the mermaid situation all over again.

"We just started building. We covered up as much as possible, moved their houses further into the woods, and stayed until they got tired of trying to get us out. We basically had to live in armor the first few weeks, but they eventually got the hint."

She could feel Lamont watching her as she shook her head, her skin flushed with embarrassment on behalf of her entire species. "You boys are the *worst!*"

"What do you mean?" Jax asked, his shoulders lifted like a kid who had no idea why his mom was scolding him.

"Jax," Lamont said gently, but Angela interrupted.

"I got this, old man. Jax, I thought they were torturing you for no good reason, not because you *stole their land!* You can't just go around taking over Neverland because it's convenient for you. Other creatures live here."

"But Peter—"

"Peter thought the world revolved around him when he was a kid. And his world revolved around fighting and proving himself. Don't you ever get tired of fighting? I know I do."

Lamont narrowed his eyes at this and Jax tilted his head, but she pressed on. "We need to apologize to the fairies."

"What!" Jax exclaimed, and Lamont laughed.

"It's only right. You kicked them out of their home and then I threatened them with imaginary poison. I am not going to leave it like this. If you won't join me, I'll go alone."

She pushed between Jax and Lamont and began her descent. She could hear Jax's protests as he and Lamont climbed down behind her.

"C'mon, Lady Pan. This is just how it is around here."

"That doesn't make it right, Jax!" she called over her shoulder. The ball of guilt rolling around her in her stomach and making her queasy wouldn't fade until she apologized to the fairies, and apparently the constant fighting in Neverland wouldn't stop unless she took matters into her own hands.

When she reached the ground and pushed through another group of Lost Boys, she could hear them behind her.

"What's going on? Where are you guys going?"

"Angela is apologizing to the fairies," Lamont said, and she thought she heard a note of pride in his voice.

"Why?" Pidge said.

"She says we kicked them out of their home," Jax replied.

"Well, didn't we?"

It sounded like Pidge, Lamont, and Jax were now following her into the woods.

"Well, yea . . . but we needed the land!"

Pidge and Jax continued to bicker as Lamont shuffled and came up beside her.

"You're doing the right thing, you know," he said, looking straight ahead.

"I don't need your approval."

"I know you don't. But I wanted to tell you anyway. I missed a lot of years of telling you I was proud of you, and I have a feeling I would have had lots of reasons to."

Angela glanced over at him as they walked, trying to figure out why this man who'd chosen to leave his child behind seemed so sad about what he missed. He wasn't looking at her, but he stood straight and smiled slightly as he walked beside her, as though he were leading her into a new school or into a concert or recital. She almost laughed at the idea of this man walking into an auditorium filled with dance moms and New Balance dads. He would have earned himself whispers and side glances with his long, dark brown ponytail, thick stubble, and thigh-length white T-shirt with tattoos peeking out of the elbow-length sleeves. He'd left his boots by his hammock that morning and seemed perfectly comfortable walking through the woods in slacks cut off at the calf and nothing on his feet. If she wasn't so mad at him, she would have wanted to know more about the man everyone else would have been judging.

They reached the spot in the woods where they'd first started feeling the bites and stopped walking.

Jax looked at her and raised his eyebrows. "Now what?"

"I guess we better tell them why we're here before they start attacking." She cleared her throat. "Um, excuse me? Fairies? Pixies?"

Silence.

"Hello? We'd like to talk to you. We don't want to fight."

Jax scoffed and Angela kicked his shin.

Then, near her ear, she heard the familiar buzzing she'd heard earlier, now realizing it must be the sound of their wings beating the air thousands of times in a second. She had to fight the urge to smack it away and clasped her hands in front of her as she tried to get her eyes to settle on the source of the noise. Her dad and the boys were shifting their heads, leaning away from an invisible something in the air, and she knew they were outnumbered.

"Look, um, friends . . ." She didn't know the right term to show respect to a fairy. "I just wanted to apologize for my behavior earlier. I had no right to—"

"To threaten us?"

Angela jumped as a small form appeared in front of her nose. She blinked, trying to focus on what was now only a spot. But as her eyes adjusted, she noticed it was a woman. She had black hair, a brown cloth wrapped around her tiny body, and clear wings beating behind her.

"Yes," Angela said. "I had no right to threaten you. I

thought you were attacking for no reason."

"Fairies are mischievous, but we are not evil. You were in our territory, and we have no reason to trust humans that come into our territory."

"I know that now, and as a descendant of Pan and a friend of the Lost Boys, I would like to also apologize for stealing your land and pushing you into the woods. These boys had no right to take your home and make it their own, and we are sorry."

At her words, the fairy lifted a tiny eyebrow. "*You* are apologizing, but you are not the one who stole the land." Her wings fluttered harder, sparkling in the light breaking through the canopy of leaves from above them as she moved toward Angela's ear to face the boys. "*They* need to apologize for their misdeeds." She said the word "they" with so much disdain, Angela wondered what else the Lost Boys had done before she'd arrived in Neverland.

Jax was kicking at the dirt and Pidge had sat down next to him. They obviously hadn't heard the fairy's request, her voice too quiet to reach much farther than the ears directly in front of her.

"Jax," Angela said, and he jumped, his hand moving to the sword at his side. "Calm down, there's no fight." His face fell. "They want you to apologize. You were the ones that stole their land, not me."

Jax opened his mouth to protest, but before he could, Pidge jumped up from the ground next to him and looked into the air, not sure where the fairies were. "We're sorry, Pixies! We're sorry for taking your land without asking!"

Angela smiled at his enthusiasm, but her face fell when

she met the fairy's gaze. It wasn't enough. "Jax?"

"Pidge just apologized!"

"I'm guessing Pidge didn't lead the expedition that pushed them off their land."

Jax scowled.

From beside her, Lamont spoke. "Angela, do you mind?" He nodded toward Jax and she shrugged.

"Jax," he said, "there's nothing wrong with apologizing when you're wrong. It's what men do."

"But Peter said men fight."

"Sometimes, when they have to. But that's not all they do. And when you've done something to hurt someone else, you apologize."

Jax stared at Lamont. He barely knew this man standing in front of him and had no reason to believe him or take his advice, but Angela could see his head nod ever so slightly and she wondered how it felt, after years of no guidance, to finally have someone help you make decisions when you were struggling. Jax looked almost relieved as he glanced up at Lamont and gave a small smile, and Angela almost laughed at the sight of the tattooed pirate giving life lessons to the wild Lost Boy.

Jax lifted his head to the trees like he was about to crow, but instead of belting out his victory cry, he ever-so-softly whispered, "I'm sorry, fairies. I'm sorry."

Angela turned to the fairy, wondering if the quiet apology would be enough to earn peace. She squinted and saw the fairy was stone-faced.

The pixie gave a small nod. "As you should be. So, when are you moving?"

"What?" Angela said. "Moving?"

"Moving!?" Jax exclaimed. "What do you—"

The fairy interrupted. "If you're truly sorry, you'll leave our part of the woods—the part of the woods you stole. The Lost Boys have many hideouts across Neverland. Presumably, you can return to one of those?"

Angela relayed the fairy's message to Jax and watched his face turn red with what she assumed was frustration and a little bit of embarrassment.

"But . . . but . . ." Jax looked from Angela to Lamont, and the wayward pirate gave a small nod.

"FINE!" Jax yelled and stalked off.

Pidge glanced at Angela, then scrambled to catch up. "Jax! It's OK! We can go to the *other* treehouse. We have so many. I like this one least of all anyway!"

Angela laughed and addressed the fairy. "It looks like we're leaving. I hope this fixes things between us?"

"Us? You act as though you are one of those wild, chaotic boys."

Angela shrugged and motioned for Lamont to follow Jax and Pidge out of the woods. "I don't really have much of a choice."

CHAPTER 8

Lamont wasn't sure why Jax had been so reluctant to leave the treehouse to venture to a new hideout. When they approached another clearing only a few miles from the one they'd vacated, it was to an almost identical treehouse complete with a hammock and firepit. It even had an overgrown trail leading down to the beach.

For the best, Lamont thought as the Lost Boys settled into

the new location, immediately resuming their games and favorite activities. They didn't want it too obvious where they were staying in case another stray pirate made their way to shore.

"You did a good job today," Lamont said, approaching Angela as she watched the flames of the fire the Lost Boys had built jump and dance into the air like the boys around it. They were laughing as they imitated Angela swinging through the air with the bug spray and celebrating what they saw as yet another victory. They didn't seem to mind the new location. But Angela didn't look like she felt like celebrating. She was sitting on a blanket, her knees pulled to her chest, her bulky sweater wrapped around her, head resting on her knees. The fire was reflected in her brown eyes—his brown eyes—and Lamont wondered if she often found herself the only quiet one, staring off into the distance, trying to see beyond wherever she was at the moment. There was so much he didn't know about his daughter.

As Lamont sat down, he followed her line of vision and realized she wasn't looking into the fire or staring at nothing. She was watching Jax, who was also taking a quiet moment to himself while the other Lost Boys laughed and danced around him.

"I think we broke Jax," she said, tipping her head toward where he was sitting.

It was true that the boy seemed out of sorts, not his usual energetic self, running around the camp, looking for the next fight. But Lamont did not believe he was broken. "I think he'll be OK. He learned a lot today, thanks to you."

"And to you," she added and then shook her head. "But

maybe it's not our place to teach him these things. The Lost Boys are happy with the way things are. They fight—it's what they do."

"And it's not what you do?"

"If you ask my mom, it's exactly what I do. It's what we both do and have always had to do . . . well"—she glanced sideways at him—"at least since you left."

Lamont sucked in a breath but held in the words stinging the back of his tongue. "But you're tired of fighting?" he asked, remembering the words that slipped so easily from her lips when she was talking to Jax.

"When your whole life is one big fight, yeah . . . . you get tired. Especially since . . . I mean, you're right. I am tired."

"Maybe the boys are too. Maybe they're tired of fighting, but they don't know any other way."

She shrugged, her eyes falling back to Jax.

Lamont swallowed, gathering the courage to say the things he *should* be saying, the things Smee had sent him here to say.

"If you're so tired, why don't you go home?" He wondered if his voice sounded as strained as it felt.

She tilted her head and narrowed her eyes and his stomach went cold. He wanted nothing more than for her to stay in Neverland, making up for the years they'd missed together, but Smee wouldn't have it.

"Do you *want* me to go home, Lamont?" Her tone was flat.

"I want you to be happy." That was the truth.

"You don't have any idea what would make me happy."

That was also the truth. "I'd like to. Why are you here, Angela?"

She rolled her eyes and stood up. "I'm going to bed."

Their moment was over.

Lamont stood when she did and watched her walk toward the treehouse and disappear inside. He sighed and turned back toward the fire. Jax was still slumped on the other side, staring into the flames that matched his hair, and Lamont made his way over to him and sat down.

"Hey, Jax. How's it going?"

The boy shrugged.

"Interesting day, huh?"

Jax looked up at him out of the corner of his eye and shrugged again.

Lamont had decided that amiable silence was better than forced conversation, when Jax spoke up.

"Do you really think that real men apologize when they're wrong?"

Lamont nodded slowly. "I do."

"Have you apologized to Lady Pan?"

The question was so blunt that Lamont jerked his head down toward Jax, and Jax jumped, still on guard with a pirate around the campfire.

Lamont kept his voice soft as he answered, "I've tried."

"You know what real men *shouldn't* do?" Jax asked.

Lamont smirked. "What's that, Jax?"

"Give up."

"So you think I have a chance at forgiveness?"

Jax's head tilted and he crossed his arms, his freckles pulling together as his face scrunched up in thought. "Lady Pan is always worried about doing what's right. When someone apologizes and is truly sorry, forgiving them is the right thing to do . . . right?"

Lamont loved Jax's easy explanation and desperately wanted to agree so that the boy could tell him that as long as he apologized and truly meant it, Angela would forgive him. But Neverland's rules were much more simple than those of the outside world.

Before Lamont could confirm or deny Jax's theory, a sound like an injured bird pulled their gazes from the fire toward the treehouse.

"What's that?" Jax asked, but before Lamont could answer, a gentle sprinkle trickled from above, as though a shower had been turned on, and Jax turned to Lamont, panic in his eyes.

"What is it?" Lamont asked as the noise came again, a combination of a hiccup and squeak that for some reason made his heart ache.

"It's Lady Pan." Jax looked at the sky. "She's crying again."

"Again?"

Jax nodded. "She does that." He made a move to stand. "What should we do?"

Lamont smiled at the boy's concern but put a hand on his shoulder to prevent him from rising. "It's OK, Jax."

"But if she's sad, we should try to help. The last time she cried, I made her smile, and then we played."

Lamont shook his head sadly and tried to fight the envy that was creeping in at the thought of this boy getting more chances to dry his daughter's tears than he'd had. "Sometimes that works . . . but sometimes people just need to cry."

"Oh," Jax said, falling back to the ground. After a moment he looked up toward Lamont. "The world is very complicated outside of Neverland, isn't it?"

"That it is, Jax. That it is."

***

When Angela woke up the next morning, something felt different. The boys, true to the claim that they didn't need a lot of sleep, were usually up before her, flitting around the camp in a general state of aimlessness. They were always up to something, but there was never any urgency behind it, never a point or a destination. It felt like Saturday morning every single morning. But today felt like a Monday.

When Angela opened her eyes, she could hear the boys moving around outside the treehouse, shouting at each other, and she could feel a sense of purpose vibrating through the air. They had a plan. She pulled herself out of her bed, and while she normally demanded a few moments alone in the mornings before anyone talked to her, today she marched straight over to Lamont, who was sitting on a log by the fire, watching the activity of the boys with interest.

"What's going on?" she asked, pulling her sweater over her T-shirt to block the early morning chill. It felt too early for anyone to be up, even energetic Lost Boys.

Lamont shrugged and pointed. "I'm not sure, but Jax is definitely planning something."

Angela followed Lamont's finger and found Jax waving his sword in the air and calling to the other boys. "Gather every weapon you can carry. Hopefully, we won't need them, but we have to be ready!"

"Ready?" Angela asked. "Ready for what?"

"I don't know, I haven't asked," Lamont said casually, enjoying the show.

"You're no help!" She turned and marched off toward Jax. "Jax! What's going on?"

"Good morning, Lady Pan! You're just in time to join us. We could use someone with some control over Neverland during our mission."

"Mission? What mission? What are you planning, Jax?"

"It's been pretty quiet since we got the pirates out of the lagoon, so we're gonna go make sure they remember who's in charge around here."

Lamont had followed Angela over to the chaos, and he spoke from behind her. "Jax. I'm not sure that's wise."

"Why didn't you try to stop them earlier?" Angela demanded of Lamont. He'd just been sitting around all morning, watching them plan an attack on the pirates, and had done nothing.

"I didn't realize what they were—"

But Jax cut them off. "Look, I know things are complicated where you two come from. I know there are always a lot of emotions flying around and people crying and people who love each other hurting each other."

Angela and Lamont both looked at the ground.

"But around here, things are simple. Lost Boys fight pirates. That's it. That's what we do. Or at least, that's what we *used* to do."

"I thought the whole point of getting the pirates out of the lagoon was so you didn't have to fight them," Angela said.

"It was to get our lagoon back. And we did. But if we just

sit back, the pirates will think we're weak. That's why they took it in the first place. We're just gonna sneak on the ship, play some pranks, torment some pirates, and then sneak off."

"Oh, that's *all?*" Angela rolled her eyes.

But Jax had already turned back to his plans.

Angela rounded on Lamont. "We need to do something!"

Lamont shook his head. "I can barely get my own daughter to listen to me. How am I supposed to get a group of rowdy boys to listen to a man they barely know?"

Angela glared. "Fine. I've managed this long without you, anyhow."

It was a low blow, and Angela knew it the moment she saw Lamont's face, but she didn't have time to worry about his hurt feelings. She turned to catch up with Jax, who was slinging a bow over his shoulder and securing a quiver of arrows next to the sword on his belt.

"Are you coming with us, Lady Pan?"

"No, I'm not, and I don't think you should go either. I think—"

"What?" Jax snapped. "Do I need to go apologize to the pirates now too?"

Angela stopped following him. "What does *that* mean?"

"It means things were a lot easier when Peter was around and not so worried about doing the right thing all the time."

"Well, I'm not Peter!"

Jax spun around so they were face-to-face. "Well, I know that now!"

Angela groaned as her face grew warm with frustration and the sky overhead began to darken.

Jax shook his head and pointed above her. "Hey! That's not fair. You can't use Neverland against me just to get your way."

"I'm not doing it on purpose, Jax!"

The sky rumbled.

"That's enough, you two!"

Angela and Jax both jumped and turned toward the sound of the unfamiliar tone. Lamont towered over them, his hands on his hips, his eyebrows scrunched together, his usually calm, kind eyes flashing. They were in trouble.

"Jax, Angela is only trying to help, but Angela, Jax is a grown . . . well, he's experienced enough. I think he can do whatever he wants but"—he sighed—"I don't really know how to do this."

"No, you're right," Angela turned away from them both. If he was on Jax's side, she wasn't going to argue. "He can do whatever he wants," she called over her shoulder. "But I don't need to be a part of it."

***

"They'll be fine, you know," Lamont spoke from where he was stoking the fire, coaxing out flames from last night's diminished coals. "This is what Lost Boys do."

Angela didn't look up from the book she was reading. She was well aware of what Lost Boys did, and she didn't need a pirate filling her in.

When she didn't answer, Lamont continued on another track. "Where did you get that, anyway?" He motioned toward the book.

At this Angela lifted her head, only because she had been wondering the exact same thing. "You know, I'm not really sure. My room, I guess? But I don't remember any books being there when I first got here. In fact, I've found a few recently . . ."

As perplexed as Angela was at the situation, Lamont didn't seem put off at all. In fact, he was nodding.

"That's not strange to you?" she asked.

"Not really, given what we know about Neverland and how it reacts to you. I've also been here long enough to see it change based on the Lost Boys. This world belongs to children, and its characteristics are unique to each child. It knows what your heart desires and it is happy to oblige."

Angela sighed. If Neverland knew what her heart desired, it would be nice if it told her.

Lamont misread her sigh. "You're really worried about them, aren't you?"

"I just don't see a need for all this fighting. If Neverland really knew what I wanted, wouldn't it find a way to stop it?"

"Well, it's also the Neverland of a very large group of very rowdy boys. If you hate it so much, Angela, why don't you go home?"

"If you want to know so much about me, why are you always trying to get me to go home?"

Before Lamont could answer, there was a scream, and Angela and Lamont both jumped and turned toward the beach.

Angela's stomach turned cold as she realized that while

Pidge had chosen to stay behind rather than torment the pirates, she hadn't seen him in a while.

"Pidge!" she yelled and ran toward the beach, already pulling Lamont's sword from its spot on her belt. She could hear Lamont close behind her.

They emerged from the path onto the beach, and Angela stopped, frantically looking around for the source of the scream. She found it on the edge of the water. Pidge was lying on his back, a pirate towering over him, gripping a sword in two hands like a butter churn. Pidge was rolling in the sand, avoiding the blade of the sword as the pirate stabbed it downward over and over. Luckily Pidge was small and fast and screaming his head off, and the pirate couldn't seem to make contact. Angela's grip on her sword tightened at the sight of Pidge so scared and all alone.

She took a step forward but felt Lamont's hand on her shoulder. "Angela, let me."

"I've got this, pirate." She had no idea what gave her the confidence to make this statement with such certainty; she only knew Pidge needed help and she'd been taught that when things were tough, she was her own best weapon.

She pushed forward, sword out in front of her, not the slightest clue what she was going to do when she reached the pirate. At the last second, when she realized she had no idea how to use the sword she was gripping so tightly, she pulled it to her side, angled her shoulder so it was leading her forward, tucked her chin to her chest, and barreled toward the pirate like a football player going in for a touchdown. She let out a guttural moan that startled the pirate enough to stop his stabbing and look up, but not with enough time to guard himself against the attack.

When her shoulder made contact with the pirate's side, it was like hitting a tank. The impact didn't do much, but it was enough to knock him off balance and make him lose his grip on his sword. Pidge rolled in the opposite direction, toward Angela, as soon as he was free. The sword fell to the sand. Continuing her first attempt ever at mimicking football moves, Angela dove toward the sword, covering it with her body, while the pirate struggled to regain his bearings. She rolled her body up just enough to find the handle of the sword and pulled it out from under her as she army crawled away from the now unarmed pirate.

She hadn't seen him approach, but from behind her, she heard Lamont call to Pidge, "Toss me your knife, boy!" She pulled herself to her feet and found Lamont approaching the pirate, who was now stumbling toward Angela.

Until that moment, it was easy to forget that her father, the gentle, soft-spoken man who followed her around trying to bond, had actually spent most of his life as a pirate. His whole body was tense as he approached his old crewmate, the small knife gripped in his hand as though he was going to stab the man's throat. And given the look in his eyes, Angela couldn't rule that out as a possibility. When Lamont reached him, he gripped the collar of his shirt in one hand, practically lifting him off the ground.

"Go back to your ship, and don't ever let me catch you on this island again."

The pirate looked for a moment like he wanted to try to convince Lamont of his swashbuckling roots, but another look at Lamont's face and the knife pointed at his neck convinced him it wasn't worth it. The pirate stumbled backward and, without another word, fell into the boat he'd brought to shore. Lamont, Pidge, and Angela didn't move until the small boat was at least halfway back to the pirate ship. As Angela watched her father keep his eye on the horizon, she wondered what type of pirate he had been to instill fear in his foe without so much as swinging a sword.

When they were sure he wasn't coming back, Pidge let out a deep sigh of relief and a nervous giggle. "You saved me again, Lady Pan!"

Before Angela could answer or celebrate their small victory, Lamont turned to face them and she froze. He was still in pirate mode and his brown eyes sparked with anger, but when he spoke, his voice quivered.

"Don't ever do that again." It was a low rumble of a request, but Pidge jumped and Angela shivered.

"Do what?" She tried to keep her voice steady, to hold onto the confidence she'd felt when she first saw Pidge lying on the beach, but it was withering under Lamont's gaze.

"Do something so stupid!"

"*Excuse* me?"

"Do you even realize what could have happened there? That was a *pirate* you charged. Not a mermaid, not a fairy, not a group of bumbling men separated from you by a ship and a lagoon—a pirate with a weapon who could have easily killed you."

"But he didn't!"

"But he COULD HAVE." Lamont's voice cracked as it rose, and this time Angela jumped. On his last words, the fire in Lamont's eye began to fade and the tension in his body receded. His shoulders slumped, his head drooped forward, and his gaze fell to the ground. When he spoke again, Angela had to step forward to hear him. "I just got you back, I don't want to lose you again."

Angela didn't know what to say, so she went with the thing that had been ingrained in her brain since her birth. "I can take care of myself."

Lamont looked up. "Do you know who you act like every time you go off on your own? Do you know who else thought they were smarter and tougher than everyone and didn't need help from anyone?"

Angela swallowed but didn't answer.

"Peter."

"I'm not Peter!"

He sighed. "So you keep saying."

CHAPTER 9

When Jax and the other boys returned, it was to a subdued trio sitting around the fire. Angela, Pidge, and Lamont stayed quiet as the boys trooped up the trail, crowing over a successful mission. When Jax reached the fire, he stopped and looked down at the silent group.

"Everything went just fine, Lady Pan. Just like I said it would."

"Great," she mumbled.

Jax hadn't yet caught on to the tension circulating around the fire. "The only weird thing is, one of our canoes was moved when we went to come home."

Angela looked up from the fire. "I'm pretty sure a pirate stole it and used it to come to the beach and try and kill Pidge."

"Oh," Jax said, his eyes darting past Angela to Pidge. "He's OK, though!"

"Yes, he's OK," Lamont said. "Thanks to Angela."

"Ha!" Jax laughed as he patted Pidge's shoulder. "Pidge should just stick with Lady Pan. She's pretty good at saving his life!"

"It's not a joke, Jax! Life and death isn't a joke!" Son of a . . . . she was going to cry again. In front of Jax, in front of Pidge, and in front of her dad.

Jax jumped at her outburst and looked at Lamont, his eyes wide and questioning.

"Angela," Lamont said softly, and she looked up as he started to move toward her.

She'd been so cruel to him ever since he arrived, so angry at him for leaving, that she'd never considered what it must be like for him to see her for the first time, only to have her push him away at every turn.

"It's OK . . . everyone is fine."

He put a hand on her shoulder, and instead of pushing it away, she was overcome by the need to be close to someone who cared about her. She missed her mom so much. She wanted to be home but couldn't go home. She wanted to enjoy Neverland, but it was so hard to watch these boys mock death every single day when she was only trying to escape it. It was exhausting trying to fight when sometimes she just wanted to give up. So she did. She crumbled against Lamont, and she heard him gasp as he slid both arms around her.

"It's *not* OK," she sobbed. "Everyone is *not* fine. I'm *not* fine." Lamont's arms tightened around her, but he remained quiet, which *was* fine. There was nothing he could say that could replace the hole shaped like her mother in her heart. But as they sat there, father and daughter wrapped in an embrace for the first time, the depth of the hole didn't feel so dark and deep.

The next time Angela looked up, her eyes were dry, and Jax, rather than running inside to get out of the downpour that had been brought on by her outburst, was waiting next to her and Lamont.

"Lady Pan," he whispered carefully, as though the sound of his voice would make her start crying again. "I'm sorry I almost got Pidge killed."

Angela snorted through her stuffed-up nose, which made Jax smile. "It's OK, Jax. Just don't let it happen again."

And then she laughed. And then Jax laughed. And then Lamont, with one arm still wrapped around her shoulder, laughed. And they all kept laughing until the clouds broke and they could see the setting suns and Lamont had to get up and stoke the fire before it was too dark to see.

***

Lamont reached the beach and glanced behind him once

more to make sure no Lost Boys had followed. He was fairly certain they'd been too engrossed in their game, and Angela in telling them why the game needed more rules, to pay any attention to the smoke billowing up from the beach.

But Lamont saw it, and he knew what it meant. He'd been told to watch for it. Luckily they'd stopped watching him so closely as they learned he could be trusted, and he'd excused himself, full of regret that he'd had to leave behind the laughter and contentment the group had found after Jax and the boys had returned from their mission. For a moment, they'd almost felt like a little family, and Lamont was happier than he thought he could be, and then he saw the smoke—and he was reminded that no matter how close Angela and the boys got, and how much progress he thought he was making with Angela, he was still an outsider.

When he reached the beach, the pirate was waiting. A single pirate, which at least told Lamont that Smee didn't expect trouble from him.

The pirate sneered, crinkling up his face when he saw Lamont approach. There were no pleasantries with pirates; he got straight to the point.

"Smee wants to know your progress."

"He hasn't given me a lot of time. I don't have much progress to report."

"He says if you need extra help controlling those boys, he's happy to provide it. *And* he says if he sees one more Lost Boy on his ship, he'll start killin'." The pirate was looking hungrily around the beach, obviously still sore about the most recent Lost Boy antics and in the mood for revenge.

"I don't need help. My plan will work, it will just take

time." But even as he said it, he knew his conviction was failing.

When he realized who had arrived on the island, he'd been just as eager as the pirates to get Angela out of Neverland, though his motivations were different than theirs. But now, with the prospect of getting to know his daughter spread out before him . . . well, he needed a new plan, one he didn't have yet.

"Tell Captain Smee to stay back or it will ruin any progress I've made. I've got this under control."

The pirate grumbled his consent but didn't move, keeping his eyes on the island.

"You can go now, mate." His words were friendly, but his hand fell to the sword sheath hanging down by his side, pushing it behind his back slightly so the pirate wouldn't notice it was empty, and stepped forward.

The pirate growled out of the side of his mouth but took a step back toward the rowboat. "Right then. I'll tell Smee." He pushed the boat off the shore into the water. "Have fun with the children," he added in a gravely singsong voice as he rowed away.

Lamont watched him until he was just a speck hidden by the profile of the looming ship and then turned back to the beach . . . and found himself chest-to-face with Jax. The boy had his sword drawn and the tip was resting just below Lamont's neck. He froze and lifted his hands.

"Easy, Jax."

"What are you trying to pull, pirate?"

He was back to being "pirate." "You don't understand. It's . . ."

"A long story?" Jax's green eyes shone in the moonlight, and Lamont saw the fire and passion only a Lost Boy could feel burning there. He'd been killing pirates for years and he was ready to do it again. "We're tired of your stories. It's time for the truth."

Lamont sighed. This boy worked hard to play, but his boyish body and appearance hid years of experience and wisdom. It seemed Neverland could keep your body young, but you couldn't hold onto the innocence that experience slowly rubbed away, like a rock on the beach smoothed by the encroaching tide.

"The truth is, the pirates want Angela gone. They want Neverland back the way it was before she showed up."

Jax snorted. "To use a word Lady Pan taught me, 'duh.' What does that have to do with you?"

"When they found out who I was, they decided I should be the one to get her to leave. I'm supposed to earn her trust and convince her to go home. That's all."

"That's *all*?" Jax stepped forward, his blade inching closer to Lamont's neck. "If she leaves, she dies. You send her home, you kill her, pirate!"

Despite the blade at his throat, Lamont twitched and leaned closer to Jax. "What did you say?" Lamont growled and Jax's arm stiffened. Lamont took a breath, trying to quiet the years of pirate instinct threatening to surface. "What do you mean, 'she dies'?"

Jax's eyes widened and the sword dropped slightly. "Oops," he whispered.

"Jax?" Lamont said. "What do you know?"

Jax dropped his sword and sighed, the words falling from

his mouth like the shooting stars that led the way to Neverland. "Lady Pan is sick. *Really* sick. Her mom sent her here to see if Neverland would make her better and it did! If she goes home and gets sick again, she'll *die*, so she has to stay here forever, which I think is kind of nice but kind of makes Lady Pan sad even though she doesn't *want* to die and she's happy she's not sick, she still misses her mom which makes her sigh a lot but she says it's possible to be happy and sad all at once . . ." Jax sucked in a breath to continue, but Lamont lifted a hand to stop him.

"OK . . . OK, Jax. Thank you for telling me." His voice was strained as he tried to talk around the buildup in his throat and chest from this new information.

He could feel Jax watching him as he ran a hand over his face, rubbing his eyes. The weight of Jax's declaration pushed him down, and he sank onto the sand, his elbows resting on his bent knees.

The boy spoke again. "You can't send her home. I won't let you hurt her."

Lamont looked up at Jax. The sun was setting behind him, and he had to lift a hand to protect his eyes from the glare that was turning Jax's form into a dark shadow.

The corner of Lamont's mouth twitched. "I thought she didn't need protecting."

"Doesn't mean I won't try," Jax grumbled, kicking at the sand.

Lamont laughed through the knot in his chest. "You're a good kid, Jax."

Jax just shrugged. "Everyone needs someone to take care of them whether they know it or not."

Lamont nodded. "You're right. And I promise all I've ever wanted to do was take care of Angela and Moira. I lost my chance with her mother, but I can still do my best with Angela."

"What are you going to do?"

"Nothing yet. The pirates know my plan will take a little time, so we can use that time to come up with a better idea."

"Why don't you just tell her what's going on? Why didn't you tell her from the beginning?"

"Did any of you trust me enough to believe something like that?"

"OK, no. But what about now?"

"You want me to tell her the pirates sent me? That she was *right* about me all along?"

"So, you're not going to tell her anything?"

"I don't think we should. Not now."

Jax laughed.

"What's so funny?" Lamont asked.

"Let's just say, it might not be smart to be without a weapon if she finds out you lied." And Jax turned to head back to the hideout, still laughing.

***

In the days and nights that passed, Lamont almost forgot why he'd left the pirate ship, the only home he'd known for most of his life, in the first place. This small chunk of Neverland, a clearing deep in the woods with a sprawling treehouse and roaring fire, felt more like home to him than the pirate ship ever had—second only to the months spent with Moira. Angela was more amazing than he'd ever thought possible, and he honestly preferred the company of the Lost Boys to the pirates. Their vibrating energy was the perfect complement to Angela's calm steadiness.

While the boys were happy playing pirates or running from the lagoon back to the treehouse all day, Angela was quieter. She could sit for hours just watching the water, and Lamont learned not to interrupt her during these moments. He knew she was thinking of home and the choice she'd made to come to Neverland. He never told her he knew she was sick and she never offered the information. In these quiet moments of her reflection, Lamont imagined Smee briefly celebrating on his ship as Neverland's suns dimmed and the trees stopped dancing. It was almost like a pre-Pan Neverland, and Smee must have thought he'd won . . . until Jax came up behind Angela and called to her to come play or Pidge ran up to her saying something sweet. Then her eyes, and Neverland, came back to life.

And so Neverland cried when she was sad, but oh how it shone when she was happy. During the moments spent splashing in the lagoon or swinging from the rope swing or racing the Lost Boys through the open fields and down to the beach, the suns of Neverland burned brighter than Lamont had ever seen, even during the days of Pan. When Neverland was at the mercy of a forever-twelve-year-old boy, it was consistently bright and mischievous. It shone over his adventures, providing enough sunlight to burn off his energy and enough moonlight to rejuvenate him for the next day. When Neverland was at the mercy of Pan, it was beautiful. When it was at the mercy of a thirteen-year-old girl, it was unpredictable.

When she was playing, it was as bright and hot and fierce as her determination to enjoy her new life and not dwell on the things she was missing. When she laughed, the blue skies practically rippled. When she and Jax fought, as they often did, Neverland was quick to take her side, and the storm clouds rolling in behind her would intimidate Jax into backing off. Angela insisted she didn't do it on purpose, but Lamont suspected otherwise.

But Lamont's favorite moments were the ones they shared together. When the Lost Boys all fell asleep, either around the campfire, fighting slumber until the very last moment, or in their rooms in the tree hideout, he and Angela often stayed around the dimming embers, dwelling on the events of the day. When their conversations turned to her home and her mother, the crisp night around them, so ripe with the possibility of their budding relationship, turned heavy. The clouds filled with moisture and the air with humidity and you could smell the rain that pooled, ready to fall. The suns and the moon performed their good night dance, and the air filled with nostalgia for a place she was sure she would never see again.

Lamont told her stories about the years before Angela was born because for some reason he was able to recall every single moment of his time with Moira, and every single story she'd ever told him. She asked about his years as a pirate, but of that, he was never as clear.

If she noticed that he stopped urging her to go home, she didn't call it out, and for that he was thankful—for that and for so much more.

When the fire died, Angela would stand and stretch, and while she never reached out to hug him, and he never expected her to, she would smile that smile that was so much like her mother's and he would be wrapped in warmth.

"Good night, Lamont," she'd say.

"Good night, Angela." And she would leave him by the fire waiting to see if it would rain.

When an hour or so had passed and the sounds of dozens of snoring and breathing children joined the night sounds of Neverland, he would stand, look around, and quietly make his way toward the beach.

Every night, he stood guard, watching the pirate ship for any signs of movement, any sign that Smee was becoming impatient and was going to try to make a move rather than wait for Lamont to deliver on his plan.

Tonight, his nightly guard duties paid off. From the beach, he saw a small boat making its way to shore. He knew they'd been sent to scout out the situation for Smee . . . to find Angela and report back on how easy or difficult it would be to come take her. But Lamont was ready to face an antsy pirate. He knew what he had to do—lie. Every day Smee didn't make a move was a little more time he had with Angela, but it wouldn't last much longer, and he hadn't yet thought of a way to both appease Smee and keep Angela in Neverland where she wouldn't get sick. And he knew he wouldn't on his own. So, when he came face-to-face with this pirate, he would lie, and then tell Angela the truth so they could decide what to do together.

Lamont stayed in the shadows until the boat slid across

the sandy shore and the pirate's boots splashed into the shallow waters. Then he stepped forward.

The pirate jumped, nearly tripping back into the boat, and pulled his sword, but Lamont didn't attack. He had no weapon, but this pirate didn't need to know that.

"Lamont," the man growled, a man Lamont knew as Dirty Dave.

It appeared Dave had not expected to meet Lamont on the beach, and he glanced behind him as though debating whether he should just get in the boat and head back to the ship. But both he and Lamont knew what Smee would do if he returned with nothing to report. He stayed where he was.

"What're ya doin', pirate?" Dave asked, and Lamont shrugged.

"Just taking a walk on the beach in the moonlight. What are you doing here, Dirty Dave?" Lamont sneered and his nose twitched. He remembered where Dave got his name.

"Ya know what. Smee's done waitin'. It's time to do some-thin' and I came ta find the girl."

Lamont nodded. "I suppose you're right. She doesn't seem to want to leave Neverland, so I guess we need to take a different course of action."

The pirate tilted his head like a confused dog.

"We need to take care of her ourselves," Lamont clarified and the pirate nodded excitedly. "But not now."

Dave's face fell. "'N' why not?"

"You weren't sent here to kill her, were ya? Are you gonna sneak into a pack of Lost Boys armed with knives and swords, some they've taken off pirates like you when they sliced 'em, and just kill her?"

Dave gulped. "Well, no. I was just gon' find out where she was 'n' tell Sm—the captain. But with you . . ."

Lamont shook his head. "They trust me and it'd be smart if we kept that trust just in case. I'm not gonna do Smee's dirty work for him, but I will deliver her."

The pirate grinned and stepped forward, but Lamont held out a hand. "No, just me. Angela trusts me. If we try to kidnap her, we risk the Lost Boys discovering us and putting up a fight. I'm her father. I can get her to come with me willingly, straight to Smee."

Dave lifted an eyebrow, considering the plan. "When?"

"In the morning. I'll deliver Pan's descendant to Smee tomorrow morning."

Dirty Dave stood for a few more moments, looking from Lamont back to the ship, wondering how Smee would take this information. Then, he seemed to decide delivering a proper plan for getting Angela was better than sneaking into a nest of Lost Boys in the middle of the night—boys who would have smelled him coming a mile away. Without another word, the pirate turned and pushed his boat into the water, disappearing into the darkness.

Lamont held his breath until the outline of the boat disappeared into the night sky and then sighed. Now, he needed to talk to Angela. But he hadn't yet turned to follow the path back up the beach when he heard the crack of a branch behind him.

He spun, his hand on his empty sword sheath, and found Angela. Her eyes were wide, darting between him and the spot the pirate had just abandoned, and her face was red.

She was gripping his sword in her right hand, but as he stepped forward and whispered her name, the sword fell to the ground, the sky began to rumble, and the clouds above them broke open.

CHAPTER 10

A s Lamont said her name, Angela's heart snapped like the twigs under her feet and the clouds opened, soaking both of them in seconds.

"Never trust a pirate," Angela's voice rose over the roar of the wind and the pounding rain. "That's what she said, and I should have listened. She knew . . . she *knew . . .*"

It was a phrase her mom had mumbled over and over

during some of her most intense writing sessions. Maybe she hadn't meant it as advice, but it was a lesson Angela should have taken to heart.

"Angela . . ." Lamont stopped when he saw her chest heaving up and down, her jaw clenched.

"I came here because I was worried about you! I didn't want you wandering around without a weapon. We *trusted* you!" she yelled, fighting to be heard above the storm of her own making.

"And you were right to," he said, stepping forward, but she shook her head and he took a step back.

"You *just* told that pirate you would deliver me to Smee!" she shouted.

"I did but—"

"It's not what you think!" came a voice behind her, barely a whistle above the rain and wind. She turned and saw Jax pounding down the path, splashing through puddles and waving his hands. "It's not what you think, Lady Pan!"

She looked from Jax to Lamont. "What do you mean? How do you know, Jax?"

"Can we please go inside and talk about this?" Lamont spoke slowly. "We can take some deep breaths and have a calm—"

"No!" Everyone was soaked now and the wind was coming at them sideways, stinging her cheeks harder with each enraged beat of her heart. "Tell me *what* is going on."

Lamont lifted his hands, "OK, OK! I come to the beach every night to keep an eye on the pirates. I watch to make sure they're not going to come to shore."

"Why would they come to shore?" Though she was sure

she already knew the answer.

"To get to you. To get rid of you."

"Why wouldn't they have tried to do that weeks ago?"

"Because I told them I could do it."

Her skin grew hot and a flash of lightning crackled just over their heads, and she heard her mom's voice, *"Never trust a pirate."*

Lamont talked faster. "I only told the pirate I would deliver you to keep him *away* from you. Once he was gone, I was going to come find you and tell you everything and we would figure out something together."

Angela shook her head. "What do you mean, 'tell me everything'? What are you NOT telling me?"

Lamont sighed. "I was sent here to get you to leave Neverland."

The ground vibrated with thunder, and Angela reached up to hold her cheeks, trying to protect them from the stinging rain.

She wanted Lamont to stop talking. She needed time to think, but he continued. "That's why I talked about your mom and home so much. The pirates wanted to kill you, so I told them I could get you to leave. But once I found out you were sick—"

"You what!?" She whipped around to face Jax, almost slipping in the wet sand, and he jumped at the sudden attention. "You told him?"

"I . . . I had to, Lady Pan! He was trying to get you to leave. He thought he was saving you by trying to get you to leave."

"And you believed him?"

Jax's face fell. Had he not considered there was another

choice? "Well, yeah. I did. He's been nothing but nice to us the whole time he's been here. He doesn't want to hurt you, Lady Pan. He wants to protect you."

"Protect me!? Protect me? I am sick to death of everyone trying to protect me all the time. I got to Neverland by myself, didn't I? I came up with the plan to get the pirates out of the lagoon. I've saved Pidge over and over. What is it with you males always feeling like you have to protect the females in your life? Why didn't you tell me, Jax? Why didn't you come to me? I thought we were friends."

"We are! That's why I didn't tell you. I wanted to—"

She sucked in her breath. "Don't say it . . . don't you dare say it."

"I . . . I didn't want to hurt you."

She sighed. "Well, I got news for you, kid. Life hurts. Sometimes you get told you're going to die before you barely get a chance to live, sometimes you get to live forever but without the people that mean the most to you in the world. And sometimes your long-lost father comes back into your life just long enough to twist the knife he shoved in your back when he left. And it all really, really, hurts."

"Angela," Lamont whispered, barely loud enough to be heard over the rain, which was now coming down at a steady drum. "You don't understand . . ." he started but trailed off again and Angela groaned.

"*What?* What don't I understand? I understand that you're the reason my mom had to work so hard, and fight so hard to have a normal life. I understand you're the reason for the sadness that always haunted her eyes and the reason she forced *me* to fight even when I wanted to give up. I understand that you thought you wanted a picture-perfect life with a nice wife and a baby, but when it comes down to it, you're just a pirate and, like she says, you can *never trust a pirate.*"

Lamont was shaking his head, staring at the ground, and at this last declaration his head shot up and he stepped toward her. She was so caught off guard she didn't move and his hands gripped her shoulders.

Jax yelled, "Hey!" and reached for his sword, but Lamont was louder.

"I didn't leave you, Angela!"

Jax froze and Angela whispered, "What?"

"I wanted to stay! I was planning on staying! Your mother *kicked me out!*" The declaration shot out of him like helium leaving a balloon. When the words were out, his shoulders sagged and when they reached Angela, the storm around them came to a grinding halt as her stomach twisted.

"No. You . . . you got cold feet . . . You . . ."

"No. I didn't. I begged her to let me stay." Lamont dropped to his knees in the sand. "I told her it wasn't what it looked like . . ."

"What wasn't?" Jax whispered.

"The note. The note stuck into my door with a sword. She saw it before I did, and she laughed, running toward it like it was some sweet gesture I'd set up for her. She giggled and asked what I was up to, but her smile faded as she read the words I'd never wanted her to know.

"*Do not fail me, Lamont. Every descendant of Pan must die. Do not forget your oath to your captain. Kill them. Kill them all.'*

She read Smee's words out loud and when she finished, she was no longer looking at *me*.

Every ounce of love that had grown between us over our months together, extinguished from her eyes in an instant and all she saw was a pirate.

I needed to make her believe that the mission no longer mattered, that I was still the man she fell in love with, so I tried to move toward her, to touch her, to tell her everything I needed to tell her without words but ..." Lamont shook his head. "As soon as I moved she jumped. She put her hands over her stomach and when she did that, when she moved to protect you from *me*, I knew everything between us was broken.

"I tried begging. I needed to make her understand, but she just kept shaking her head. She was hurt, she was scared, and she was doing what she felt she needed to do to protect her unborn baby. And then she said it.

'Just go. Go back to your captain and don't ever come near me or this child again.'

"It was over. She knew, just like you do"—he motioned to her and Jax—"what pirates are capable of, and she knew the history of Hook kidnapping her mom and uncle. There was nothing I could do. So I left.

"I came back to Neverland. I lied and told Smee there were no descendants left that still believed in Neverland, even though your mother believed more than most. Whoever he sent back to leave that note must have never seen your mom or figured out who she was, because he believed me. I went back to being a pirate, knowing that, at the very least, you were both safe."

As Lamont's words faded, the storm around them also quieted. Lamont looked around at the dark sky, and the still trees, and then back at her. He looked almost relieved that the wind and rain had faded, but the storm had died because part of her also had. That part that trusted her mother unconditionally was gone. The fire inside her that burned when her mom said they needed to fight because they had no other choice was now extinguished. She hadn't been abandoned. She'd sent him away.

"Angela?" Lamont said when she'd been quiet for a few moments. "Your mom never let me prove her wrong. She never let me show her that pirates can be kind and trustworthy . . . but you knew me as a pirate from the beginning. I've never hurt you or the Lost Boys. I've done everything I can to keep the pirates *away* from you. You *know* me."

But Angela shook her head. "That's where you're wrong," she whispered. "I *thought* I knew you. I thought you understood that I never needed you to protect me. You could have told my mom you were a pirate from the very beginning instead of lying to her. You could have told me the plan and we could have worked together. You claim we never trusted you, but you never trusted *us*. You wouldn't trust us with the truth. You didn't lose your family because you're a pirate. You lost your family because you *acted like a pirate*."

Lamont winced, but Angela didn't care. Her entire existence was a lie, thanks to this man. He didn't deserve anything from her.

"Angela, please. Don't do this. Don't push me away like your mom did."

"No! You don't get to ask anything of me. You've lied to me

from the moment you stepped foot on that beach and I'm done with it. Go back to your captain."

Lamont recoiled at her mother's words, but Angela turned away only to find Jax blocking her path to the trail.

"You don't get to make that choice!"

"What?"

"You don't get to just kick him out. You're not Pan!"

Angela groaned. "You're right! And I never wanted to be!"

"Just let him stay." Jax's voice cracked for the first time since she'd known him, but at this point, Angela's heart felt like stone.

"No," she said flatly. "Lost Boys don't lie to each other." She lifted her eyebrows at Jax. "Or at least, I thought they didn't."

Lamont was shaking his head over and over, but Angela couldn't watch. She didn't want to see the droplets streaming down his cheeks even though the rain had stopped. As she started to walk back toward the treehouse, she squared her shoulders and lifted her chin. She heard Lamont try her name one more time, but she inhaled deeply and kept walking. When she was a safe distance away, she exhaled and the flow of tears she'd been holding back escaped and the rain that had been waiting in the heavy clouds let loose. As the tears and the rain flowed, they washed away any urge to run back and cry in Lamont's arms while she forgave him for everything. Life was too short—or too long—to spend it with people you couldn't trust.

***

"Didn't Lamont say he would deliver the girl himself, Captain?"

"That's what he *said*, but do you believe him? That codfish couldn't do the job the first time. I was an idiot to think he could do it this time. Fathers can't be trusted to do the job of pirates. No, he's not going to deliver her. It's time to do what we should have done from the beginning."

Lamont sat on a ledge on the outside of the ship, listening to the exchange between Smee and Dirty Dave.

When he'd left Angela and the boys, he didn't rejoin the pirates, but he had returned to the ship. He spent the night clinging to the outside of the vessel, waiting for them to make their move . . . and now they were.

"What's that, sir?" asked Dave, and Lamont rolled his eyes.

"Take care of her, you dolt! We're pirates! We don't sit around and wait for one of our lot to do our work! We do our killin' ourselves!"

A crowd had gathered around Smee, and they cheered at the word "killin'." They were bored and bloodthirsty and willing to follow their captain anywhere, no matter how inept he might be, because that's what pirates did in Neverland.

"I'm done hatching plans and strategies and *waiting*. Smee waits for no man! I'm done with this sunshine and I'm done with happy Lost Boys!"

The pirates surrounding him gave an agreeable growl. They weren't happy that Angela had invigorated Neverland or that the Lost Boys had resumed their favorite activity of torturing the pirates. Jax had told him, out of earshot of Angela, about the times they'd snuck on the ship. While the pirates snoozed in drunken slumbers they stole their weapons, raised the sails, and lifted the anchor so the pirates awoke to find their ship in a new position. Lamont would have rathered the boys stay ashore, as their pranks only invigorated the pirates, but he had to admit he laughed at their antics when Jax described the pirates' reactions.

Now the pirates were done with pranks and energetic Lost Boys.

"It's time to take back Neverland, men! Tonight, we go ashore, and when those boys are sleeping, we attack. No kidnapping. No clever plans. No battle of wits. Just a good ol' fashioned slaughter to show them who Neverland really belongs to!"

The men cheered and roared and stomped their feet, and Lamont knew there was no more time to sneak on and try to convince Smee to abandon his plan. The men were in on it now, and they were itching to swing their blades and cut the boys who had been torturing them for weeks. It was time to head back to shore, to the Lost Boys, and to Angela. If he couldn't stop this battle, he would at least fight on the right side of it.

Just as Lamont shifted his weight, ready to scale the side of the ship and drop into the water, his nose twitched as a rancid stench filled the air around him. He heard the rattly breath of one of his former shipmates as they chuckled. He looked up and found the dirty face of Dave glaring at him over the side of the ship, an almost toothless grin pulling at the grime-filled cracks in his filthy skin.

"Well, what do we have here? A bilge-sucking traitor.

Captain! Captain Smee, looky wha' I found! When was the last time we used the brig?"

CHAPTER 11

Angela sat in Lamont's hammock, reading. The fire was out, the treehouse was quiet, and she was alone. She hadn't been truly alone since first coming to Neverland, and it was something she secretly craved every single time she stepped out of the treehouse to find herself face-to-face with Jax suggesting an adventure or Pidge just wanting to talk. Today, no one had talked to her. There was no Lamont pestering her about her past or her mom, no buzz of boys running in circles around the fire or pretending to kill pirates or reminiscing about when they'd actually killed them. Even Neverland seemed quieter. The sky was gray and the air felt thick so that anything that moved, moved slowly, including her.

When Jax came walking up from the beach a few minutes later, he barely acknowledged her and she tried to push down the longing for his excited greeting of, "Hey, Lady Pan! What should we play today?" She was constantly telling him she didn't always want to play, that sometimes she just wanted to sit and be quiet, a response that caused his head to tilt to the side and his shoulders to rise to his ears. He'd let out a giggle and ask, "What's the point of that?" before running off to grab a boy more willing to play than this girl was.

When he stopped in the middle of the clearing and looked around, his eyes falling on a small knife near the fire pit, Angela couldn't help herself—the quiet was too loud and his silence hurt more than anything he could possibly say.

"Where is everybody?" she asked quietly.

Jax didn't look up but reached down to the grab knife. "On the beach, waiting for Lamont to come back. Pidge forgot his knife and we didn't want anyone to be unarmed in case there's trouble."

"What makes you think Lamont will come back? He's a pirate. They're all the same."

Jax winced. "That's what I thought too . . . until we met him." All of a sudden he lifted his bowed head, and his green, watery eyes met hers. She started at the sudden emotion in his voice when he yelled, "Why are you doing this?"

"Jax, I didn't—"

"You made him leave just when we all started liking him."

"He lied to us! He lied to *you*."

"He was just trying to help you!"

"I don't need—"

"Sometimes you do! Everyone does!"

Angela jumped out of the hammock, not sure if she wanted to turn and run away or shove him to make him stop talking. "You don't understand!" He'd been in Neverland so long, what did he know about the hurt of the real world and the gut-wrenching pain when someone you thought you trusted betrayed you?

"I'm still *human*, Lady Pan! I know hurt and sadness. We all left your world to try to escape, to run away, but it always seems to find us . . ."

His voice trailed off, and with it so did every remark Angela had planned. She'd never seen Jax's fire so dim, and the part she played in smothering that flame suddenly overwhelmed her.

"Jax, I . . ." But she couldn't finish. She didn't want to fight, but she didn't know what to say to make things right. She couldn't stand to see the look in Jax's eyes, the way his shoulders dropped forward instead of pulling back proudly. She didn't know what to say to the boy whose flame she'd extinguished, so, like her mother and father before her, she gave up and walked away.

"Lady Pan!" She heard Jax call, but she couldn't face him. She needed a second. She needed to breathe. She needed to let the events of the last few hours soak in, but at the same time, she wanted to block them out. Jax's words were echoing in her head, *"We all left your world to try to escape, to run away . . . but it always seems to find us . . ."* and mingling with the words her mother whispered just before she'd sent her here, *"I just need you to be OK."* She most decidedly was not OK. She'd tried to escape the pain and fear of death, but hurt and sadness had found her. She'd been trying to fight fate, but she was just so tired.

She leaned forward and placed her hands on her knees, trying to catch her breath, to slow the cyclone of thoughts spinning in her head before Neverland caught on to her current state and produced a true cyclone. "Focus on the breath," she told herself, trying to utilize the tools her regular yoga practices had taught her, but she'd always been really bad at this part.

The sounds of Neverland were still trying to break into her meditation when she heard something else. Voices. Had the other boys come back from the beach? Her stomach jumped and for a brief moment she thought, almost hoped, that Lamont had chosen to ignore her wishes—like a normal father—and come back.

She stood up and headed back to the clearing. But as she approached, she knew immediately it wasn't Lamont. She heard a small, high-pitched whine and instinctively swatted at her ear. But the sound didn't come from next to her. There was a fairy suspended in front of Jax, and even though it was usually hard to hear their voices if you weren't close, Angela didn't have to strain to make out what she was saying, because the pixie was holding a small cone made of a leaf—she'd made a megaphone.

"Where is the girl?"

Jax, who looked skeptical about having a one-on-one conversation with a fairy, motioned in the direction Angela had headed and shrugged. "I'm not sure." He opened his mouth, presumably to call her name, but the fairy cut him off.

"There is no time. I will tell you. The pirates are planning an attack on you for this evening. They want the girl and they're done waiting. That's all we know."

"How do you know that?" Jax asked.

"We have been watching the pirates since the apology of the Lost Boys. We thrive when Neverland is at peace and we want it to stay that way. The girl was kind to us, so we wanted to offer this warning."

Pidge and Tank had come up from the beach at the end of the conversation.

"The pirates are coming," he told them and then paused, turning back to the fairy. "Thank you," he said quietly, "for the warning."

The fairy nodded. "You must protect your friend."

Jax laughed and Tank and Pidge giggled uncomfortably. "We don't protect Lady Pan." His voice lowered. "And she gets really mad when we try."

The boys around him murmured their agreement, and instead of being mad that they were all standing around discussing her fate, Angela laughed. She laughed so loud that the boys stopped murmuring and all heads started twisting and stretching to see where the source of the laughter was coming from. She dropped the baggage she'd been struggling with off her shoulders and stepped out from behind the tree, her hands on her hips.

"I don't need these boys to protect me!" She put her hand at the sword at her hip and turned toward Jax. "If the pirates are coming, we need to be ready."

"We're ready!" Jax exclaimed, brandishing his sword, and the other boys shouted their agreement.

But Angela shook her head. "We can't just sit and wait for them to show up. We need a plan."

"The plan is to fight!"

"Yes, we're going to fight, but we need to be careful."

"Careful!? It's a fight!"

Angela almost laughed at how quickly they'd fallen back into normalcy, and she would have if the situation hadn't been so serious. "Jax. From what I've seen, Smee is someone we need to treat carefully. He's impulsive, which makes him dangerous. We can fight impulsive with planning. Where do you think they'll be coming from?" she asked.

Jax pointed toward the beach.

"Are you sure?"

"Yea, they're not smart enough to try and come from another direction."

"Fair. OK, then we need to know *when* they're coming. We need someone small enough to hide in a tree and signal us when they're headed this way."

There was a buzz and a small burst of wind against her face, but she shook her head. "No, we need your help with something else, if you're willing."

She felt a tug on the side of her shirt and looked down to find Pidge looking up shyly at her. "I can do it, Angela."

"Pidge, are you sure? It's really high and you'll have to be really loud when you see them coming. Can you warn us without them knowing what you're doing?"

Pidge nodded, his thin lips pursed together. "I can do it. I want to do it."

"OK, Pidge. I believe in you. When we tell you to, head to that tree, crawl all the way to the top until you can see the beach, and wait."

He nodded and she turned to the rest of the boys who'd wandered back up from the beach when Jax hadn't come back and were now waiting patiently for her to give them orders. Warmth blossomed out from the pit of her stomach at the sight of them. She'd never tried it, but she imagined that this flash of heat followed by overwhelming contentment must be what it was like to take a shot of hard liquor. They weren't tilting their heads at her in confusion or searching the skies behind her to figure out where she came from. They weren't looking from her to Jax, or even Lamont, unsure who to listen to or who to trust. They weren't raising their eyebrows doubtfully as she cautioned them against making any rash decisions. They were simply waiting. They were looking at her with wide, trusting eyes, their hands resting on their weapons. She had to fight the sudden urge to wrap them all in a big hug, and she reached up to stop a small tear from falling down her cheek. But apparently, these boys had learned something during her stay in Neverland, and from beside her, Tank reached over and gripped her wrist. "We know, Lady Pan. We know."

On her other side, Jax took her hand and squeezed it. "It's OK to cry sometimes," he said with a sniffle, and she smiled through her blurred vision.

Before she could catch her breath and gather herself long

enough to give an order or share a plan, the air was pushed out of her and a small form collided with her stomach, wrapping thin arms around her waist.

"We believe in you, Lady Pan!" Pidge exclaimed. Then his chin dropped to his chest and he looked up sheepishly through wide eyes. "And we . . . we . . . we love you!"

She laughed through her clogged throat and pulled the back of her wrist across her eyes. "That's enough, all of ya...we don't need a rainstorm right now!"

She was truly proud to call these boys her friends and at this moment very glad to be in Neverland, but . . . something was missing.

"Jax," she said, "do you suppose Lamont knows the pirates are coming to attack?"

He looked down at the ground and she knew it was because he didn't want to give the answer he had ready. If he'd returned to the ship, he knew their plan . . . and he hadn't come himself to warm them.

"You're right." She nodded. "He probably went back to his real family. There's nowhere else for him to go, right? If he's not with us, he's a pirate. And we all know what Lost Boys do to pirates."

Jax lifted his gaze, no longer as enthusiastic about fighting and slicing pirates. "But—"

"No, he chose his side." She gripped the weapon at her hip, the sword she rescued from the beach when Lamont hadn't made any attempt to come back. The sword she'd wanted him to have until she found him plotting against her and then hadn't had the heart to get rid of, even when its owner never came back.

She swallowed against the ball forming in her throat and fought back the rage that would bring storm clouds upon them. There wasn't time for that. Not yet.

"OK," she said, pulling the sword out and lifting it into the air, "let's fight some pirates, shall we?"

***

Less than an hour later, the sun was setting on Neverland. Pidge was in his tree, the Lost Boys were scattered through the woods, and she was crouched on the roof of the treehouse with Jax waiting for their cue.

"Lady Pan, do you really think Lamont chose to join the pirates again?"

"Well," she said, keeping an ear on the situation below, "he's not here, is he?"

"No, but . . . what if something happened?"

She swallowed. She hadn't considered that. But no. She shook her head. "Lamont's a grown man. He can take care of himself. He left when my mom found him out, and he did the same thing to us. We don't need him."

She heard Jax sigh next to her. "Right. We don't need any more men around here who might leave again."

She winced. She hadn't realized how much the situation with Lamont mirrored what happened with Peter. That's what Jax had meant by hurt and sadness finding them . . .

"I'm sorry, Jax. I wish things were different."

"It's OK," he said, and then smiled. "We have you . . . Angela."

She laughed. "Hey, you called me Angela."

He shrugged. "Well, you're not just a lady version of Pan. In fact, you're almost nothing like him. You're brave like him, sure, but sometimes he could be selfish and a little mean. He didn't see himself as anything but our leader for a very long time. You're you. You're Angela, and you're our friend."

She smiled as she realized Jax had forgiven her for her mistakes and that, no matter what happened between them, they would always be OK. But before she could even get out a thank-you, they heard it. It was a caw that wasn't quite a caw. It was the sound of a new species of Neverbird, a NeverPidge, and it was squawking like it was being attacked by a swarm of fairies. But of course, it wasn't, not yet.

"That's Pidge," she said, crouching lower and inching toward the edge of the roof toward the rope and where she could see the forest floor below. "They're coming."

All was quiet for a few moments and then came the rustle of leaves, the cracking of breaking branches, and the thumping of dozens and dozens of boots against the ground.

"They're here," Jax whispered, and the line of trees broke and those footsteps turned into forms that were dingy and snarling and waving swords and shouting to each other . . . but one voice shouted louder than all the rest.

"Wipe out any Lost Boy that stands in your way, but find me that girl!"

Smee was not at the front of the group but hidden by four or five looming figures, figures she imagined he'd chosen specifically for hiding behind. Jax noticed it too and she heard him whisper, "The coward."

The men ducked and pushed their way into the treehouse, and she could hear them grunting through halls that were much too narrow and bumping their heads on ceilings that were much too low. The other noises she heard made her cringe. As they entered each room, they would growl and she could hear their swords swish through the air, meeting the raised forms they thought were the bodies of Lost Boys. She didn't know why she was so surprised at how casually they went about killing these boys in their sleep, but there were goose bumps on her arms as she gripped the rough rope in her right hand, keeping as still as possible.

She heard the exclamations and swear words as each realized they had not just etched another kill into their belts. They heard them shuffle out of the treehouse, back to where Smee was waiting, and tell him, "They're not there, sir. Not a one of 'em."

Smee was quiet for a moment. He didn't swear or scream like she expected, just bowed his head. When he looked up, his eyes flashed with anger. "The traitor Lamont."

"But we've got Lamont, sir."

She looked at Jax, wide-eyed. Lamont didn't rejoin the pirates. He'd been captured. Jax narrowed his eyes as if to say, "Told ya."

"Well, somehow they knew!" Smee screamed, kicking the dirt.

"Now what?"

"Now, we wait. They have to come back eventually, and when they do, we'll be here." Smee ordered a number of the men to stand guard around the perimeter of the hideout and to the others he said, "Get comfortable, men. We're not going anywhere tonight."

It looked as though "get comfortable" was their favorite order so far that night, and they immediately took it to heart. One pirate plopped down in the hammock Lamont had been sleeping in, another spread out on the porch of the house. Another found the tire swing, and the rest sat cross-legged on the ground. The only one left standing was Smee.

This was it, she thought, looking to the woods. This was the moment.

"What do we do about Lamont?" Jax whispered.

"The plan stays the same."

The other boys wouldn't move without her signal. She looked down at Smee, who was sipping from a small rum bottle he'd pulled from his pocket and kicking at the dirt. His sword was still sheathed at his side and he looked bored. She watched his eyes dart around the Lost Boys' territory, and she thought about him sneaking up behind two of them and slitting their throats. She thought about him sending Lamont to come to her world to kill her mother and thought about his hatred of anyone related to Pan. As these thoughts swirled around in her head, a breeze began to swirl around the pirates. At first, it just tickled their cheeks and a few even relaxed into it, but then it began picking up branches and leaves and someone yelped as one hit them in the eye.

The breeze turned to wind and the wind brought in a storm cloud that dropped large droplets of rain. The men didn't move, they didn't mind the rough weather, but many were now focused on shielding their faces, and Smee had moved closer to the house where his view of the woods was obstructed. The first bolt of lightning was the cue. As the thunder that followed rolled, the roar of the Lost Boys pouring from the woods was drowned out and the pirates didn't notice them, even after the first man, the one in the hammock, was killed. The hammock kept swaying in the breeze while its rider stared blankly at the cloudy sky.

It was only after a few of his men crumpled into piles onto the ground with Tank's arrows sticking out of them that Smee noticed something was wrong. "What the—?"

But the men relaxing on the ground were overrun by Lost Boys, and before many of them could stand, they met a sword across their chest or a knife in their gut. Angela cringed, glad she was up on the roof. For all her talk about plans and strategy, she was no pirate killer.

"I can't believe you can just kill them," she said to Jax.

"They don't think twice about killing us, so we have to."

Half their ranks were gone before they even realized they were in a fight, and when the first pirate finally pulled his sword, Jax stepped to the edge of the roof and crowed, letting reinforcements know they were ready for them. The Lost Boys who had been engaged in battle heard Jax's call and hit the deck, while the pirates, confused, looked up to see what they were hiding from. They squinted through the wall of rain but couldn't see what was coming until it was upon them. There were yelps and curses, and swords fell to the ground as the pirates tried to guard their ears and faces. The Lost Boys took this opportunity to land their killing blows and even more pirates fell as the fairies swarmed.

Smee wasn't fighting but was standing on the deck of the treehouse hopping from one foot to another like an impatient child. "What are you doing, you fools? Fight them!

They're children!"

And then the first fairy reached him and he swore loudly.

Angela felt Jax tap her shoulder. It was time for the next phase of the plan.

Taking a deep breath, she scooched back to the rope swing, gripped it in both hands, and stood.

She turned to Jax. "Are you ready?"

He nodded. "Once you let go, I'll come down after you. I'll follow you, fighting off any pirate that comes close." He added a warning. "Don't look back."

She nodded. They knew the plan. Now it was just about execution.

"OK," she said. "Here I go."

"Good luck, Angela," he said.

"You too," she said, and she pulled back the rope and bent her knees to get ready for her swing.

But before she could move into action, a gruff voice called out from below, "Captain! I got one, Captain! This lil' pixie pest just squealed on her friends!"

"What are you blathering on about?" Smee asked, smacking at the back of his neck.

"Was the pixies that warned the boys, 'twas! I squeezed her till she was about to pop and she told me!"

"Oh, it was, was it? Well, I'll teach you what happens to fairies that meddle in the affairs of pirates." Smee cupped his hands over his mouth, "All together, men! Repeat after me; 'I do not believe in fairies!'"

"No!" Jax yelled, but his shout was barely audible over the chorus of pirates now shouting, "I do not believe in fairies!"

Jax put his hand on Angela's shoulder. "We have to do

something. They're helping us! We can't just let them all die!"

"No," Angela said, swelling with pride at Jax's concern for the fairies. "We can't. What do we do?"

Jax's eyes scanned the situation below and then his gaze fell on the swing. "Let me go first. I'll rally the boys. Most of the pirates are too distracted to fight right now. We'll do what we need to do, and when the fairies are revived, you come down and I'll cover you. Don't show yourself until I'm ready to cover you."

Angela nodded and handed the rope over the Jax. "You can do it, Jax. I believe in you."

Jax smiled and lifted his eyebrows. "Don't believe in me, believe in fairies!"

And with that he wrapped himself around the rope and stepped off the edge of the building, swinging swiftly to the ground below. No sooner had his feet hit the ground than he dropped the rope and pulled his hands together in a feverish round of clapping.

"Lost Boys, clap with me! Save the fairies who helped us in battle! Drop your weapons and clap your hands!"

The Lost Boys were standing with weapons raised, ready to strike any pirate who pushed past the distraction of the fairies, but when they heard Jax's call, their eyes fell to the ground, now littered with the bodies of fairies, falling one by one with each call of disbelief from the pirates. They knew how to save them, but it meant laying down their weapons.

Angela saw the hesitancy cross their faces but only for a moment. When they saw their leader abandoning both his weapon and the plan they knew so well, they sprang into action. Exposing themselves to attack, they came together for the creatures that just a short time ago they'd shown such disregard for. Their clapping began to echo through the clearing, and any boy with a fairy nearby knelt next to the tiny body, desperately clapping and drowning out the chorus of pirates with chants of, "I do believe in fairies! I believe!"

Angela's heart swelled at the scene below as she thought back to the moment Peter had saved his dear friend Tink and the desperation with which she'd always clapped when her mother told her the story and encouraged her to help Peter save Tink from across worlds. Well, she wasn't worlds away anymore.

With a rush of love for her friends and the beautiful creatures of the land around her, Angela sprang to her toes and pulled her hands together, shouting with Jax, "I believe! I believe!"

The warmth and excitement swelling from her center rolled out around her, and Neverland took her cue, lifting the voices of the Lost Boys on a breeze and carrying them through the forest, drowning out the killing calls of the pirates.

Below, fairies began popping up from the ground, a gentle buzzing slowly joining the calls of the Lost Boys. Once Jax knew his friends were clapping and the fairies were reviving, he pulled his sword.

"Keep clapping, boys! Till every last fairy lives!"

Glancing up at Angela, he lifted a finger to indicate she should wait a little longer, and in a flash he was weaving through pirates, using the butt of his sword to strike any that got in his way or seemed ready to attack a distracted

Lost Boy. In a moment, he was in front of the pirate who'd grabbed and squeezed the tattling fairy.

"Drop that pixie!" Jax yelled, aiming his sword at the pirate's neck.

The pirate looked to his captain for guidance, but Smee was too busy trying to figure out why his pirates' voices weren't louder than those of the boys.

"Yell louder, you yellow codfish!"

The pirate holding the fairy shrugged and released his grip, sending a shower of glittering dust into the air. Once the fairy was free, Jax turned back to Angela and gave a nod.

This was it. It was her turn.

Swinging through the air, she let out a crow she knew could be heard across Neverland and landed with a thud before picking herself up and breaking out in a run. She didn't pause—she knew Jax would find his way to her.

As she ran, she could hear shouts as the pirates realized who had just whizzed by them and knew she wouldn't have much of a head start.

"That was her!" Smee yelled amid the confusion. "After her, you fools!"

The forest floor behind her exploded with footsteps as any pirate left standing started to run. She heard a grunt and a shout that confirmed Jax was behind her and taking out anyone he could along the way.

"Right behind ya!"

With Jax behind her, pirates behind him, and Lost Boys behind them, she pushed her legs to go as fast as they could and headed toward the lagoon.

Maybe it was Neverland helping her out, but she could

swear she felt lighter than she ever had, and it felt as though her feet barely touched the floor on each landing. She moved swiftly over fallen logs and dirt piles, barely slowing to scale them. She wasn't worried anymore about whether she could outrun the pirates but about how Jax was doing fighting them off. But she didn't turn to look; she'd promised she wouldn't. Any hesitation could result in them catching up and overpowering her, and even with her sword, she wouldn't stand a chance.

She reached the cliff where she'd first caught sight of the lagoon and turned toward the trail that scaled the rocky wall. As she neared the water, she began to shout.

"Pirates! The pirates are coming! The pirates want the lagoon back, you must fight! Fight for your home!"

As she shouted, ripples began to form in the calm water, and it only took a moment for heads to break the surface.

The mermaids looked around, saw her running and the group of pirates behind her, and their beautiful faces morphed as their eyes narrowed and their features sharpened.

"Pirates," she heard them hiss as they disappeared below the surface. When they appeared again, they were armed, and she had reached her destination—the rock where she'd stood to fool Smee. She ducked behind the rock as arrows began to fly through the air, knocking down pirate after pirate. She only hoped their aim was true and the arrows would continue to find her foes and not her friends. With the pirates distracted, Jax turned his attention from the one he'd been fighting, who was immediately struck in the side by an arrow, to where she was waiting at the base of the rock. He met her where she waited, and he crouched, forming a step with his hands. He lifted her to his shoulder, and she used that to step, crawl, and shimmy to the top of the rock.

With the Lost Boys coming at them from one side and the mermaids firing arrows and throwing spears from their other, the pirates were cornered, outnumbered, and dropping like flies. From her perch, she could see a man in a long red coat not engaged in battle but crouching with his hands over his head, crawling across the beach, trying to stay out of the action. She shook her head, more and more surprised at the incredible cowardice of this supposed "captain." How he and his crew had managed to capture Lamont was beyond her. Her stomach flipped, and she winced as she thought about Lamont sitting on that ship alone, convinced she and the boys had abandoned him, thinking that his only child hated him. She glanced around the beach where the boys and the mermaids had the battle with the pirates under control and saw, out of the corner of her eye, an empty boat just out of reach of her rock.

No one was looking.

If she sprinted, she could make it to the boat without anyone seeing her, the boys could finish the battle with the pirates, and she could sneak onto the ship while they were all distracted and save Lamont. She could hear Lamont's voice in her ear, *"How could you do something so stupid?"* But what choice did she have? She could do this. She had Neverland on her side.

She glanced down below her rock. Jax was engaged in a fight with a pirate, his swordplay skills far surpassing that of the man in front of him. He would be OK. The same was true for all the boys. She didn't need to protect them; they'd been fighting battles like this for years.

"You're so strong," she could hear her mother whisper. *"You don't need anyone."* But this time, Angela shook her head at her mother's voice; it wasn't true. She needed her father.

In a flash, Angela was on the ground and sprinting across the sand, toward the boat closest to her rock. Smee was hiding somewhere on the beach and the other pirates were too distracted to notice. Reaching the boat, Angela gripped the side and pushed it away from the beach. Splashing through the water to catch up with it, she grabbed the side and jumped in. She'd given it some good momentum and it slid easily out into open water. Before she turned to grab the oars, she saw Jax on the beach. He'd seen her. His eyes were wide and a little hurt—she'd abandoned their plan and gone off on her own, just like Peter would do, but he didn't dare yell her name or call attention to where she was.

As she watched Jax get smaller and smaller in the distance, something changed on his face. The hurt melted away and was replaced with fear, and when he rushed toward the edge of the water, screaming her name, she knew something was wrong, even before she heard the voice.

Goosebumps erupted on her neck and arms as she felt a hot breath in her ear.

"'Ello there, *girl*."

Chapter 12

"Bet you didn't think ol' Smee could outsmart the brilliant descendant of Peter Pan, eh?" Smee was downright giddy that he'd pulled off such a cunning plan, sending another pirate to the beach in his coat and hiding in the boat closest to where he'd seen her climb the rock. "I knew you couldn't pass up a chance to save yer dear old daddy, and I knew if you were anything like Pan, you'd come alone."

He laughed and Angela rolled her eyes. She couldn't believe she'd let *this* pirate outsmart her. He'd told her his plan three times since taking her sword and pushing her to the bottom of the boat.

"Everyone underestimates me, but all of Hook's best plans were mine. That's what they never tell ya."

Angela would be more annoyed by his bragging if she wasn't so worried about what he was actually capable of. Maybe she *had* underestimated his cunning, but he was still unpredictable and that was even scarier.

She felt the boat bump the side of the ship, and Smee stood, grabbing her shirt and pulling her up so the blade of his sword was inches from her neck. A rope ladder hung down the side of the ship in front of her.

"Climb, girlie. And no funny business. I've killed plenty a Lost Boy and I've got no qualms about killing a little lost girl."

As Smee's words hit her in the back, the air was sucked out of her lungs as though he'd punched her. Lost girl. It wasn't the worst insult he'd flung, but as the meaning settled over her, any adrenaline coursing through her body at the thought of finding the right moment to escape was sucked out of her. When she reached the top of the ladder, Smee gave her a hard shove from behind to keep her from gaining steady footing while he finished his climb. She didn't scramble to her feet. She waited for him to tell her where to go.

She was still on the ground when he emerged above her and he grinned. "There's a good lass." He grabbed her shirt and pulled her to her feet, once again placing his sword across her chest . . . but he needn't have bothered, she wasn't fighting back.

"Not as cocky without your daddy and an army of boys at your disposal, eh?" He pulled her toward one end of the ship and paused. "Now, where should we kill you? The brig is taken." He winked.

Through her gloom, Angela felt a small rush of warmth. At least Lamont was alive. Smee pulled her toward a set of double doors. "This will have to do for now." He opened one and shoved her into what appeared to be a bedroom. "Too nice for a Pan but seems appropriate to kill you here." He paused and aimed his sword toward her, narrowing his eyes. "What's wrong with you, girl?"

Angela had collapsed to the floor in the middle of the room, her chest heaving as the truth of what was about to happen washed over her. This was it. She'd fought so hard to stay alive and now she was going to die. Hot tears stung her eyes and she only briefly worried about crying in front of the man who was about to kill her. It clearly wasn't the typical reaction of his average victim, and Smee seemed momentarily stunned. Well, what did he expect?

She pulled her knees to her chest, and without any regard to Smee or what he thought, she let the tears stinging her eyes fall down her cheeks and soak her pants. After all she'd been through, after everything she'd done to survive and all the sacrifices she and her mom had made, she was going to die here . . . on a pirate ship, in a gaudily decorated captain's quarters, thousands (or it could have been millions) of miles away from her mom. She'd come here to live, and now she was going to die. Alone. It served her right. She'd thought she was so independent, so strong. She hadn't needed help or company, or anyone to take care of her—and now her wish had come true and where had it gotten her? She really was just a lost girl . . .

Angela hiccuped at the thought, and out of the corner of her eye saw Smee jump.

"Stop that," he grumbled, his sword paused in midair. "This isn't how this—Oy!" Smee lurched forward, losing his grip on his sword as the floor under them tilted and then settled. Smee looked at the still open doors behind him to the deck and swore. A storm was raging outside and the ship was not prepared for it. Smee looked from the storm to her and back again, swearing under his breath, cursing the crew that was fighting on the beach and not available to help him secure the ship.

"Get yourself together and be ready to face me like a man," he grumbled at Angela before turning and running out onto the deck, the double doors slamming and locking behind him.

Angela looked up. Smee was gone and she was still alive—but for how much longer? She looked around the room, taking in her situation. If only she'd let Jax in on her plan, she would have an ally. If only she hadn't run Lamont off.

She groaned, pulling herself to her feet and drying her eyes, her chest still heaving with anger, embarrassment, and self-pity. Why couldn't she just admit she needed help once in a while? Her mom had been strong to the point of stubborn, and look where that had gotten her, left raising a child alone without one of the sweetest and kindest men there ever was. Angela sighed as she thought of the time she'd gotten to spend with Lamont, and how much of it she'd squandered being mad or annoyed. He was her *father*. If it was OK to need anyone, it was OK to need your *father*, even if he wasn't perfect.

She sobbed again and heard Smee yell from the deck as the wind picked up and a clap of thunder broke. She'd lost everyone because she refused to ask for help and now there was no one to ask. It wasn't hard, she thought, and then, to prove it to herself, yelled, "Help! Please!" She didn't have any trouble screaming it into empty air, and if her father was here, she would tell him too.

"Dad?" she shouted, trying out the word for the first time. "I need you, Dad! Please help me! I need help! I need my dad!"

"Angela?"

She gasped and jumped to her feet.

"Angela! I'm here, sweetie! Are you OK?"

She followed his voice toward the wall to her right. "Dad! Lamont, I'm here! I'm OK. Keep talking!"

"What are you doing here? What happened? Are the boys OK?"

She smiled through her tears at his concern as she traced the wall with her hands, trying to figure out where his voice was coming from. She found a grate in the floor and knelt down. It must have been connected to the brig.

"They're OK . . . or they were when I saw them last. Oh, Lamont, I'm sorry. I did something stupid. I wanted to find you, to save you. I didn't ask for help, I just jumped in a boat and Smee was there, he was waiting. It was a trap. He knew I would come alone because Peter always tried to do everything alone. You were right, I'm just like him. I'm—"

"Shhh . . ." His voice traveled up through the grate and stopped her rambling. "Angela, don't. It's OK. You're just determined . . . and stubborn. Like your mother. Everything's going to be OK."

"But how do you know? We're trapped!"

"Because you're not alone anymore. I'm right here, and if you hadn't asked for help, you would have never known. That's the difference between you and Peter—growth. It was only when he decided to grow up that he truly became a man, but he fought it for so long because he was afraid." He fell silent and Angela sat back against the wall, savoring the fact that he was so close. He was right. She wasn't alone.

After a few moments simply enjoying the presence of each other, Lamont broke the silence.

"Angela"—his voice danced up from below—"why are you in Neverland?"

She answered without hesitation, "To always be a little girl and to have fun."

There was a moment of silence and then he asked again, "Why are you *really* here?"

Angela sighed. Could parents always tell when you were lying, even if you weren't raised by them? Even if you weren't in the same room as them? "To cheat death, I suppose."

"Why?"

"What do you mean, why? No one wants to die."

"Those who are scared of death don't want to die. You don't strike me as the type to be afraid."

"Everyone is afraid of something."

"That's true. But I don't think you're afraid of death. So

what are you really afraid of?"

When asked the right question, Angela gave the answer that had been sitting on her chest for as long as she'd been in Neverland. "I am afraid of dying, but not because of what it will do to me. I'm afraid of what it will do to my mom. I don't want her to be alone. I didn't want to leave her like you left her. At least if I'm *here*, she knows I'm alive somewhere. She knows I'm fighting for my life."

"Is that what you want? To just be alive *somewhere*?"

She knew he knew the answer to his question, so she didn't bother to answer.

He didn't push her but instead said, "Angela, your mother is strong. She always has been. I didn't want to leave, but I knew when I did that she would be OK. I know with all my heart that she doesn't want to lose you, but I also know that no matter what happens, she will be OK."

Angela sniffled, wiping the tears off her cheeks. Lamont had no way of knowing what his words meant to her, that they were exactly what she needed to hear . . . but maybe that was the wonderful thing about fathers.

They sat in silence again for a few moments before she finally broke it. "Dad?"

There was a pause and then his voice cracked. "Yes, Angela?"

"I don't want to die here."

"Then let's get out."

Lamont started speaking faster, his voice lower and his tone urgent. "Listen to me, Smee will be back soon." Angela swallowed but shifted closer to the grate so she could hear everything Lamont was saying. "The weather calmed, but I bet you anything he's drinking right now to build up some nerve. He kills his men, but killing kids has never been his strong suit. This means he's going to be . . . susceptible when he comes in."

"Susceptible to what?" Angela didn't think she could get away with convincing him she was Pan again.

"Anything really, but in this case . . . the supernatural."

***

A few minutes later, after a quick search of the quarters, she sat in the corner of the room, wearing a black, wide-brimmed hat perched atop a black wig with tight curls, and a red coat with gold fringe and buttons. She was swimming in it all, of course, but she'd pulled the curtains and dimmed the lights, leaving only a single candle burning nearby, casting shadows, and Lamont had assured her that if they played it right, it wouldn't matter.

"Pirates are very superstitious," he'd told her.

"Enough to believe in *ghosts?*" she said skeptically.

"Enough to believe in ghosts. But when Smee sees Hook in the corner, it won't matter what he believes. He was afraid of Hook when he was alive, and he's been haunted by his reputation and presence every moment since he died. Hook never truly left Smee, and it won't take much to convince him that's who he's seeing now. His inferiority complex is our best weapon. Just let me do the talking."

So Angela waited in the corner of the bedroom that used to be Hook's and was now Smee's. Maybe it was because he was so afraid of Hook, but the bedroom seemed more like a shrine to the former captain rather than Smee's living quarters. A thick coat of dust covered intricately designed candelabras, ostentatious statues, and gold drinking goblets. The only things that gave any indication that the bumbling Smee lived there were rum bottles by the unmade bed and some of his clothes scattered about. The rest was all gaudy elegance and captain-like order. It had made it easy to find the clothes she needed, still neatly organized in an unused wardrobe. It also made it easy to believe that when he stepped through the door Smee would believe Hook had come back to once again take residency of his room.

Lamont was waiting by the grate for the first sounds of Smee who, he said, would not enter the room quietly. He was right. The door slammed open, and it was a good thing Angela was hidden under so many layers because she jumped.

"Oy!" Smee called through the darkness. "What's the meaning of this?" He stumbled into the middle of the room, and Angela could see Lamont had been right—he'd been drinking. "Where are ya, ya pint-sized wench? Ya can't hide in here." He slammed the door behind him so that anyone trying to escape would be trapped. But she wasn't looking to run away.

"The only person who ever tried to run from trouble, Smee, was you." A muffled voice rose from the shadows. And while Angela recognized it as Lamont, he'd adopted a slight accent, the lilt and lift of a man with a proper upbringing, and the dripping disdain of someone who was constantly disgusted by the world around him. She couldn't be sure but imagined it was a damn good impression of

Captain James Hook. Judging by Smee's reaction, she was right. Smee froze dead in his tracks. He hadn't yet noticed the figure in the corner and was looking wildly around for the source of the voice . . . but for the first time since Angela had met him, he stayed quiet.

"What's wrong, Smee, ya filthy excuse for a bilge rat? Aren't you happy to see your captain?"

"Ca–Captain? But th–that's . . ."

"Impossible? Mmm, if only that were true. I *was* resting peacefully, free from Pan and those brats and the constant headaches of Neverland and captain hood, but you ruin everything, Smee."

"M–me?" Smee was looking into the air, convinced he would find Hook floating there, looking down his long nose at him.

"You brought a girl aboard my ship, you codfish!"

"But it's . . . it's *my* sh—"

"Fool!"

Smee jumped.

"The *Jolly Roger* will always belong to Captain James Hook."

Smee was still looking around for the source of the voice, and Angela could see his skepticism beginning to build. Smee wasn't a complete idiot, and he wouldn't take the presence of his captain as truth without a little more proof.

"You're not real . . . " Smee mumbled, his stutter fading, but his voice still unsure, unwilling to anger even the *spirit* of his captain.

"I am more real than your pathetic attempts at leading my crew! You're not a captain, you're a lily–livered blathering tommy cod, a sorry excuse for a bricklayer's clerk."

Angela saw Smee wince and knew his bruised ego was fighting against his logical side . . . and winning. Barely moving, she turned her head toward the candle she'd lit nearby, and as Lamont barreled insults at Smee, berating his attempts to captain the *Jolly Roger* and replace its *real* captain, Angela puckered her mouth and gently blew air toward the flame.

"You're a heathen, Smee. And such a terrible pirate you forgot the curses that befall any ship that dares bring a woman aboard. I've said it before, and I'll say it again . . . I have never in my life encountered a stupider man than you, Smee—you, empty-headed poltroon!"

At these words, the air from her lips met the candle and it flickered, disturbing the shadows of the room and at last drawing Smee's attention to her corner. It didn't matter that she was shorter than the captain, or that his clothes hung limply over her body. Just the sight of his hat and the silhouette of his curls turned Smee into the blubbering assistant he'd been for so many years.

"Oh my dear, dear Captain! I've disgraced you!"

Smee fell to his knees, years of worry and carefully disguised impostor syndrome finally catching up with him as the words of his beloved captain washed over him.

"You have always been a disgrace, Smee, 'tis no surprise to your captain to see your failures pile up around you."

"You're right, sir. Of course, you're right." Smee sobbed, dropping his face into his hands and hiding from the scornful gaze of the venerated Captain Hook. "I am no captain . . . no captain a'tall . . . ," he continued to cry, and Angela wasted no time.

While his eyes were covered and his sobs drowned out any sounds her movement might make, she closed her fingers around the handle of the sword that Smee, in his brief moment of pride, had forgotten he'd left in his shrine to his captain. She slowly stood, letting the hat and wig slide off behind her and leaving the coat sitting stiffly in the chair, as though it was still occupied by the ghost of Captain Hook.

She inched toward Smee, the sword gripped in her hand, but as she grew closer, she turned the blade so that it was pointed toward the sky and it was the hilt that made its way toward Smee's skull. In the second before it made contact, Smee looked up. Realizing he'd been embarrassingly fooled once again by a wannabe Peter Pan, he closed his eyes a split second before the sword made contact with his head.

The disgraced captain crumbled into a pile on the floor of his quarters. Angela paused, waiting to see the rise and fall of Smee's chest, and then gave a small crow of victory, signaling to Lamont that the plan had worked.

"He's down, Dad! We did it!" She bent low toward Smee's limp body. He was snoring now, lost in the unconscious sleep of drunks, and he wouldn't notice as she patted his pockets carefully, searching for a set of keys that would hopefully unlock the brig. When she found them, she said a quick "thank you" to the unconscious Smee, and let out a hearty laugh at the situation, before running to the door to find the brig and her father.

✳✳✳

When she found the cell where Lamont was being kept, Angela threw open the door and, forgetting everything they'd said to each other on the beach, jumped into his arms as though they were a normal father and daughter reunited after a long absence. Is this what it felt like for regular girls when they saw their dads after a long day? This overwhelming sense of relief and feeling of safety when their arms wrapped around you, blocking out the world and any danger? Or was that only when you'd just faced death and pirates together and come out OK on the other side?

Either way, she pressed her face against his chest and felt the pressure of his arms around her back, and sighed. When she pulled back though, she bowed her head.

"What is it, Angela?" he asked.

"I couldn't do it," she said, picturing the rise and fall of Smee's breath as she left him on the floor. "I couldn't kill him. I know I should have, but I just couldn't."

Lamont shook his head and put a hand on top of her head, ruffling her hair. "I'm glad you couldn't. Now let's get back to the boys."

And together they left the *Jolly Roger*.

Chapter 13

When Angela and Lamont reached the beach, it was to a wall of Lost Boys running toward them and supine pirates scattered across the moonlit beach.

Jax reached them first. "Lamont! Lady Pan! You're alive!"

Angela laughed with relief. "So are you!"

Jax took a step back to survey the damage and nodded. Not all of the pirates were dead, but without their leader, and with so many of their number slain, they had no reason to keep fighting. They sat with their arms on their knees and their heads bowed, awaiting orders from an absent captain. Jax didn't seem worried about them and was more concerned about what had happened on the pirate ship.

He turned back to Angela. "How did you get out?"

"It was Lamont's brilliant plan," Angela said, filling them in on the charade that had outsmarted Smee.

"Angela made a very convincing Hook," Lamont said, laughing. "What about you all? You seem like you've done well."

"It was no trouble at all! This lot has gotten soft under the charge of Captain . . . SMEE!"

The last word was shouted just in time. Lamont and Angela spun around to find a soaking wet Smee inching closer to them from the water's edge. Lamont pulled Hook's sword, the one Angela had given him as they left the ship, but Smee already had his drawn. He looked exhausted after his swim, but his eyes were fiery and humiliation burned on his face and spurred him forward.

"Out of my way, traitor," he said as though he expected Lamont to just step aside.

"Not a chance, Smee. You and your men are defeated. It's time to go before things get worse."

"I've come to take care of the girl."

"What a coincidence. That's why I'm here too." Lamont stepped forward and Smee lifted his blade to block Lamont's blow and the battle was on.

Angela stepped back, watching anxiously. Just as she thought about stepping in, or asking Jax and the boys to simply pounce on Smee, there was a tug on the back of her shirt, and as she jerked back, an arm wrapped across her chest and she felt the cool blade of a sword graze her neck. She froze, knowing any movement would push the blade farther into her skin.

From behind her, the pirate holding her shouted, "I got her, Cap'n! The girl! I got 'er!"

She knew what would happen before it did. As soon as Lamont heard what the pirate was shouting, he paused his swordplay and turned to find Angela. Smee took advantage of his distraction and brought down the butt of his sword on the back of Lamont's head. Lamont fell to the ground and Angela shouted. But Lamont wasn't down, just stunned and swaying on his knees.

Smee stuck a foot on his opponent's back, pushing him the rest of the way to the ground. "Stay down or the girl gets it!"

Lamont lifted his head. His eyes met hers and she silently asked if he had another brilliant plan. The look on his face told her he did not.

"Bring the girl here," Smee said, motioning toward her captor. "I want to kill father and daughter together. I suppose I owe them that small favor." He laughed, and the pirates who had slowly started to gather when they realized their captain was back joined in. None made a move to fight, though, as each was matched by a Lost Boy with an outstretched blade, and they were seemingly gun shy from their last interactions.

Angela, pushed from behind by the pirate, began to shuffle through the sand, slowly approaching Smee and Lamont.

She dragged her feet as much as possible, slowing their journey while trying not to draw attention to her defiance. As she crept forward, she looked around the beach, desperate for another clever solution that would save them from the clutches of death yet again. She begged Neverland to send help, something to protect them—and that's when she saw Jax. He had his sword at the ready, prepared for battle but not sure where to strike first . . . and he wasn't alone. Besides the Lost Boys standing vigil at the sides of the pirates, he had a friend dancing above his head, her wings glistening in the sunlight, a shower of gold raining down from her onto Jax's head.

"Jax!" she yelled, catching his eye and lifting her eyebrows toward the fairy. "Trust Neverland!" Her punishment for her call was a shove to her back that closed the distance between her and Lamont and Smee, but as she stumbled forward onto the sand, she saw Jax look up, searching for help from Neverland and realizing he was being covered with a fine coat of sparkling dust. He looked back down at Angela and grinned. Just as she wondered what Jax's happy thoughts would be, there was a resounding crow and Jax's feet left the earth.

All heads turned toward the crow, but their searching gazes were met with a dark streak darting through darkness, as Jax, the boy who'd earned the trust of the fairies, danced through the air in a floating waltz worthy of Peter Pan. His celebration was short, and with a twist, he shot toward the pirate guarding Angela. As he zoomed over him, Jax's foot met the pirate's head, and any threat of a sword across her neck was removed.

Knowing the leverage of his captor was gone and assuming his attention was elsewhere, Lamont shot up from the sand and spun around to face Smee, his fists balled as though ready to engage in hand-to-hand combat. But there was no need. Smee was gone, already stumbling his way down the beach. Jax could have caught him. The Lost Boys could have run after him and reached him easily, but Lamont laughed, a booming "Ha!" that made all the boys turn to see what was funny. "He doesn't realize what's awaiting him is worse than what he just ran from. Pirates have a lot of creative ways to deal with deserters."

Even as he spoke, some of the least injured pirates were pulling themselves up and grumbling, shaking their heads and motioning in the direction Smee had headed.

Above them, Jax rose higher into the night, a silhouette turning somersaults in the spotlights shining down on him from two full moons. Those below him on the beach applauded and a grin stretched across his freckled face.

Angela laughed. "Jax! Come down!"

"I don't think I want to! Ever again!"

"Well, I can't thank you properly for saving my life while you're way up there!"

Jax landed with a thud in front of her. "Oh, you don't have to—"

But she wasn't going to be stopped. She threw her arms around her first Lost Boy friend and planted a kiss on his rosy cheek. "Thank you, friend."

Jax didn't say anything, just stood frozen with a hand on his cheek, and his nose crinkled as though he'd just smelled something strange. She tried not to take offense as Lamont laughed.

"You caught the kid off guard." He patted Jax's shoulder. "You'll be fine, Jax. We owe you a debt of gratitude."

Jax still hadn't spoken when they heard a high-pitched squeak from overhead. They all turned and saw Pidge, who must have finally shimmied down his tree and made his way down the path, running along the edge of the cliff wall and waving, the early dawn light illuminating his path.

"I'm coming, guys! I can help. I'm on my way!"

She smiled at his enthusiasm, knowing the worst of the battle was behind them, glad she'd thought to make him the lookout and keep him safe in the tree, away from the worst of the danger.

"Hey, Pidge!" she yelled, waving. "You did a great job!"

He smiled and skipped at the praise, pausing his descent down the path to stop and put his hands on his hips. "I did?"

Angela laughed. "Yea, Pidge! You were . . . Pidge!"

There was no amount of flying or planning or clever tricks that could stop what was about to happen. No matter how fast anyone flew, it would be too late. No matter how swift the arrow or how quickly drawn the pistol, Pidge's fate was sealed the moment the pirate appeared behind him, sword already drawn.

Pidge's eyes went wide. His tongue met his top teeth as a stuttered "L . . . La . . ." fell from his lips, and little Pidge, the smallest and sweetest of the Lost Boys, died with the words "Lady Pan," trying to escape with his last breath.

As he fell forward off the edge of the cliff, eyes still open but the life already floating out of his body, flying through the air of Neverland as Pan once had, the cowardly pirate who snuck up behind him laughed and yelled, "I got one!"

His laugh seemed to shake the foundation of Neverland and rise up from the vibrating ground into Angela's legs, arms, chest, and finally into the space behind her eyes. She didn't move. She didn't scream, she didn't cry. She stared at the space where Pidge had just stood, empty now save the gloating, disgusting pirate, and she felt his laugh burst into a thousand pieces behind her eyes—a thousand knives stinging her brain and her heart and threatening to bring her to her knees. The only reason she didn't fall was the steadying hand gripping her shoulder. Through the echoes of the laughter bouncing around in her head, she could hear her name, but she couldn't acknowledge it. She could hear only that pirate's laughter, and it burned. It burned as her chest began to rise and fall. It burned as she grabbed the wrist of the hand on her shoulder and held on for dear life. It burned as she closed her eyes and watched the life leave Pidge's eyes over and over.

She didn't know it was happening, but suddenly her legs and arms and face stung as much as the knives banging around inside her head, and she realized the wind was picking up. Above the laughter in her head, she heard a rumble. The ground *was* vibrating, not from the echoes of the pirate's celebration, but from the thunder now rolling in from the ocean. There was no rain. The sky remained as dry as her cheeks, but there was wind, lifting the clothes and hair of the pirates and of the Lost Boys rather than drenching them. She opened her eyes and saw the panic on the face of the pirate who was still standing dangerously close to the edge of the cliff. The thought of Pidge alone up there in his last moments, no one to hug or make sure he wasn't scared, dug into her heart and snapped the taut cord that had been pulling in the wind and thunder. It snapped in a flash of lightning that hit the ground behind the pirate and made him jump and lose his balance and pitch forward off the side of the cliff to the rocks below.

When she turned, it was to find her dad and all the Lost Boys staring at her, but she wasn't done. She was still gripping Lamont's wrist and the laughter inside her head was now replaced with the voice she would never hear again—"We love you, Lady Pan!" said the tiniest Lost Boy, the only one brave enough to say the words. "We believe in you!" So small but with the most faith.

You shouldn't have died, Pidge, she thought as she fell to her knees, still holding onto Lamont. He fell with her and kept his hand on her shoulder, right where she needed it. He didn't say anything, just let grief wash over her and all of Neverland.

As the wind picked up to match the strength of her pounding heart, any pirate not dead began to stir. Anyone hiding emerged and anyone waiting for Smee to come back stopped waiting. Their ship and the boats that would take them to it were just behind them, on the other side of the lagoon, and they began to stumble through the sand, over their fallen comrades, and make their way toward them. It was every pirate for himself as they stepped over bodies and pushed each other out of the way.

The boys began to cheer at the retreat of the pirates, seeing it as a victory despite the loss of their friend, but Angela still wasn't done. Most of the men were already piled into the boats that would take them back to their ship when Smee came screaming back down the beach yelling for them to wait, to turn around and come back for their captain. When no one did, he dove into the water and began to swim.

Angela stared at their destination, the massive ship on the horizon, and thought about all that it represented. Years of terror for various Lost Boys, fear, death, men who put very little value to human life and cared only about their own pleasure. As some of the boats began to reach the ship, she thought about Pidge and his mother, and the joy on his face only moments before he'd fallen. As her heart swelled for the little boy who would never know what happened to his own mother, or get to give her or the world a proper goodbye, the water surrounding the ship also began to swell. As her anger was replaced by grief and that grief began to wash over her, the waves offshore began to rise, lifting the ship with them. Some of the men climbing aboard fell as they were pushed off balance by the rocking of the ship. Others held on and got aboard, and those still in the small boats stopped rowing and gripped the edges for dear life.

The boys behind her seemed to realize what was happening, and the harder the boat rocked, the louder they cheered, and their cheers gave her strength, and her strength gave the waves and the wind power. Now rather than just swells, real waves began forming and breaking against the ship. There'd been no time to prepare the ship for a storm, so it didn't fight like it might have otherwise. In the water, Smee was now just a speck, rising and falling with the motion of the waves. The closer he got to the ship, the harder the waves pushed him back. It was Smee's plan that had taken Pidge, it was his reign that pulled a veil of terror over her days in Neverland. Smee would not be boarding the *Jolly Roger*.

Angela was losing steam, but Neverland knew her heart and the land of eternal childhood took over for her. As she watched the horizon and Smee's progress toward the ship, Neverland read the storm raging inside her, and just beyond the ship rose the biggest wave yet. As it rolled toward the vessel, gaining strength and height, it towered over the sails, and she knew Neverland had a plan bigger than she did.

As she fell back into the sand and her father caught her in his arms, none of them could look away from the water. The wave Neverland and Angela had created together was roaring under its own power now and there was no stopping it. It took only a second for it to overtake the ship, falling over it like a blanket and pulling it down into the water as it crackled and splashed. The ship disappeared from view, as did the few remaining rowboats and the speck in the water that had been Smee. Neverland pulled them all down into the depths, and when the wave broke . . . they did not reappear.

As the roar of the water and rumbles of thunder died down, they were replaced by the deafening silence of dozens of dumbstruck Lost Boys. They'd been cheering only moments before, but now they were waiting. Waiting to see if the pirates would reappear. Waiting to see what life would be like in Neverland from here on out. Waiting to see if the disappearance of the pirates would bring back their fallen friends.

After a few moments, there was a whisper. "They're gone," Tank said.

Angela's chest was rising and falling, and there were beads of sweat across her forehead. Her dad's arms formed a hammock in which she was resting, and in her exhaustion, she couldn't tell if she sensed relief or anger in Tank's voice. The longer the ship stayed below the water, the more she wondered what the boys were thinking about a pirate-free existence.

When it was clear it wouldn't be coming up again, she started to apologize but was having trouble finding her voice. "I . . . I . . ."

Her dad touched the back of her head, trying to tell her it was OK, but before she could get anything else out, Jax crowed and she let out a relieved sob.

"The pirates are gone! Neverland is FREE!"

The boys erupted into whoops and cheers and celebrations, and she looked to her dad to get his reaction. He was smiling from ear to ear, looking back and forth from her to the dancing Lost Boys, never once glancing back to the water or to the pirates that had once been his family.

CHAPTER 14

Angela sat on the edge of the cliff overlooking the lagoon, the spot where Pidge had fallen and spent his last moments alive . . . and alone. Her feet dangled over the edge and the water stretching out before her was calm. All of Neverland had been calm since the pirates had disappeared, calm and quiet. The Lost Boys were used to losing their friends to the pirates, but Pidge's loss was especially hard,

Jax had told her. "He only wanted to take care of us."

Angela had never lost a friend to the pirates, so the whole thing was new to her. She'd never really lost anyone until the moment she'd left her mother behind to come to Neverland. She didn't know what it was like to have someone taken away before you'd had a chance to say goodbye. She'd never experienced the void of things left unsaid, but Pidge had. He'd left his home without saying goodbye, and he'd left the world with her name left unsaid on his lips.

"Hey, Lady Pan."

She looked up to find Jax sitting next to her. She hadn't heard him approach or even sit down. "Back to Lady Pan?"

He smiled. "For old time's sake."

Old times, she thought. The day she first came to Neverland felt like ages ago. Something had shifted after Pidge's death, and even Jax felt it.

"I can't stay here, Jax," she whispered and heard him sigh.

"I thought you might say that. But if you leave . . . won't you"—he tried the grown-up word on for size—"die?"

"Being here doesn't mean I won't die. Just look at Pidge."

"But the pirates are gone now—that won't happen to you."

"But something else could. Time catches up with everyone, Jax. You can't run from the world, and I can't run from my fate. I miss my mom. I almost died without her yesterday. I almost died without saying goodbye. I won't end up like Pidge. I won't lose my mom like he lost his. I would rather spend the little time I have left with her than spend a lifetime without her."

"Angela."

At the sound of Lamont's voice, she turned. His shoulders were slumped forward, and he looked like someone had just punched him in his stomach.

She stood up. "I'm sorry, Lamont. But you had to have known this was coming."

"I know," he said, his voice shaking. "You're right." He nodded, biting his bottom lip. "You should spend this time with your mother."

"Dad," she whispered, stepping closer to him and taking his hand. "I wouldn't have the strength to do this if it wasn't for you. You reminded me that I'm not afraid of dying."

Lamont's breath escaped in a long, slow exhale, and she squeezed his hand.

"Thank you," she said. "For everything."

He squeezed back but didn't respond.

She heard a groan from behind her and turned to find Jax kicking at the dirt. "Everyone's always leaving—Peter, his kids, you . . ."

"I'll miss you too, Jax."

He looked up, hurt and anger hiding the sadness sparkling in his green eyes.

"I thought you were one of us. I thought you were a Lost Boy."

She put a hand on his shoulder. "I am *not* a boy, and I am very much found. I know exactly where I belong."

He smirked a little from behind his wet cheeks. "Then you're lucky."

She looked from her dad to the group of Lost Boys who had gathered behind him and smiled. "I know I am. And so are you. Because I'm not leaving you, not really. I'm leaving you with a little piece of me." She stepped back so that Lamont and Jax were facing each other.

"Dad," she said, and he lifted his gaze from the ground. "I know you've only ever wanted to take care of me, and I'm really sorry that you couldn't. But there are a group of boys here that could really use a good man in their lives."

Lamont looked at Jax and then turned to the group of boys waiting behind him. He smiled as they kicked at the dirt and looked at each other, smirking their agreement.

"If they'll take me, I would be honored to stay here with these Lost Boys."

"Jax?" she asked. "Is that OK?"

Jax shrugged but nodded at the same time. "I guess that would be OK."

She laughed. "*Boys*," she said, rolling her eyes. "Well, I guess it's settled then. I'll go back to where I belong, and you will all stay here together . . . right where you belong." She turned to Jax. "Now, how do I get home?"

"The same way you got here, I suppose." He looked to the sky and then back to her.

"But I'm out of fairy dust," she told him.

He glanced above her head and winked. "Trust Neverland."

Angela looked up and was greeted by a buzzing sound that, when you really listened, sounded a little like a bell.

"Thank you for bringing peace to Neverland," came a small voice in her ear, and Angela giggled as a shower of fairy dust tickled the back of her neck.

Jax stepped forward. "Goodbyes are so sad. Will you have a hard time thinking of a happy thought?"

She glanced behind her to the Lost Boys surrounding Lamont and her heart swelled. As she turned back to Jax, she saw down into the waters of the lagoon below and noticed the mermaids had surfaced, their hands lifted in goodbye.

Angela shook her head. No, she wouldn't have any trouble finding a happy thought. "Not at all, Jax. Not at all."

She stepped forward, and before he could stop her, she reached out and grabbed his hand and squeezed.

He didn't jump or blush, he just smiled sadly. "Goodbye, Angela."

She smiled and touched Jax's red, freckled cheek once more before turning to Lamont. She stepped forward, paused for a second, then closed the few feet still separating them and threw her arms around his neck. His arms circled her waist and she sighed, melting into his warmth and trying to take in the scent of grass, oak, and sweat. It wasn't the sweet smell of lavender, but it was a mixture she swore she would never forget.

Her face was pressed to his chest, her cheek against the rough fabric of his jacket, when she realized she could already feel herself slipping away. Her feet were no longer pressed into the soft earth as she squeezed her eyes shut, trying to take in every sound, every smell of the world that had tried to save her life.

The arms around her squeezed harder, enveloping her, trying to hold her there, but as she thought about her father and their days together in Neverland, the salty smell of the nearby water was replaced with a hint of scent that made her heart swell.

As she thought of her mom and the home she'd missed

so much, the rough fabric of her father's jacket smoothed and softened, and somewhere in the distance, dancing like a whispered breeze, she heard a familiar voice, "Burn clear and steadfast tonight . . ." The pressure of his arms around her remained, but her own arms felt weightless as the fairy dust did its job and Neverland sent her home.

This time there was no icy, dark sky dotted with thousands of stars twinkling like fairies. There was no sea of black spreading out before her. There was just warmth and comfort as though a soft blanket were being wrapped around her.

As the cool and gentle breeze faded, she whispered into the growing darkness. "Goodbye, boys . . . goodbye, Dad. Goodbye, Neverland."

"Goodbye, Angela."

AN END

From the desk in her daughter's room, Moira stares into an open notebook, begging the words that have always brought her so much comfort and joy to come and do their work now. But the blank pages taunt her and the silence of the room is too much.

She stands and paces, missing Angela so much it hurts. Her publisher wants another book, and she desperately wants to return to Neverland, to escape the pain of the last few years, but her head is filled with her daughter and the battles she's been fighting for so long. Moira knows Angela is tired, even though her daughter would never say it. Moira prays she is not afraid. She is strong, and she is brave, but death is scary. Saying goodbye is scary.

But Moira knows, as she looks at the bed and then the window, that it was always *her* who was most afraid. Angela always faced her fears, until Moira made her run from them. Outside the window, her eyes catch a star burning and blinking brighter than all the rest. She focuses on that glow, digging back in her mind to the literature that inspired her own words, and tweaking the line slightly, whispers, "Dear nightlight, protect my brave little babe. Burn clear and steadfast tonight."

She knows Angela doesn't need protection, she doesn't need extra strength. What she needs is to know that it's OK if she doesn't want to *use* that strength. That sometimes being strong means no longer running, no longer fighting; it means letting go. It's a lesson Moira never got the chance to teach her.

And then she hears something. A rustling, a shifting of bedsheets, and a small sigh. Her breath catches in her throat before she can turn around. It's been so quiet for so long, could these signs of life actually be real? And then she hears it, a sweet voice mumbling the same word over and over. She turns to the bed and rushes to her side. Is she really back?

But as she leans forward, Moira hears what Angela is whispering and her heart freezes.

"Goodbye," she mumbles, "g'bye . . ."

She's ready.

"Angela? I'm here. It's OK, I'm here." She grabs her hand.

Angela's eyes flutter open, and when she sees Moira, she smiles weakly. "Mom?"

"It's me." She leans closer, her daughter's voice a barely audible whisper.

"Mom, I found it. It was beautiful."

Moira nods, encouraging her to go on. She never wants to forget what could be their last moments together, so she grabs the notebook from the desk and smiles at her. "Tell me."

And in those sweet moments, Angela is herself again, smiling and laughing as she talks of her adventures, her Lost Boys, her Neverland . . . and her father. She holds Moira's hand the whole time and squeezes when she speaks of the boy who never got to say goodbye to *his* mother and the father who gave her the strength to greet death. She looks fearful when she tells her about the dangers she faced and how she knew then that she didn't want to die so far away from home, didn't want to live if it meant a life of running. Her tale is beautiful and sad and Moira has never been more proud of her.

"I fought. I swear I did, Mom, but I couldn't stay. I missed you. I wanted to be with you." A tear slides down her cheek, and Mo brushes it away with her thumb as Angela looks up through heavy-lidded eyes. "And Dad said you'd be OK without me . . . You will, won't you? You'll be OK?"

Moira nods, trying to speak around her clogged throat. "Yes, Angela. You don't have to fight anymore. I'll be OK."

As she says the words, she feels the tiny body relax next to her, releasing everything she'd been holding onto for so long.

Angela sinks deeper into the bed and whispers, "No more fighting . . ."

Moira leans closer and puts her head on the pillow next to her daughter's, pulling her feet onto the bed and wrapping her body around Angela like she did when the girl was little and couldn't sleep. Her body is warm.

Mo presses her lips to her ear. "Just rest now, my darling. You're OK. You can rest."

Angela's eyes close, and like a soft wind off the ocean, she whispers, "Goodbye, Mom."

The great-granddaughter of Peter Pan wasn't killed by a pirate's sword. She didn't die running from her fate or trying to hide from death. She died on her own terms, in her own time, and when the last breath finally left her body, her skin smelled like a cool breeze on a hot summer day.

The End

THANK YOUS

Out of all the chapters and paragraphs in this book, I dreaded writing this page the most. There are so many people who have helped me on my creative journey and supported me throughout the years and I, as a writer, am an absent-minded individual so will inevitably forget someone who deserves recognition. But the beautiful thing about all the amazing people in my life is that they will not be offended. They will not hold my faults against me and for that, I am eternally grateful.

Because I cannot thank every single person who has helped me on the path to bringing Angela to Neverland, here are just a few special thank-yous to the people who have been deep in the trenches with me.

To all the writers who brought Neverland to life before me, this book would not be possible without you. Thank you for sharing these characters and this world with all of us.

To my partner in life, my foxhole buddy: Thank you for your never-ending support, and just the right amount of pushing. I'll be forever grateful for the day you said, "Oh there you are, Alli."

To G: Thank you for always giving your honest opinion.

To my best friend: Thank you for ... everything. There will never be enough words or acknowledgment pages to thank you for your proofreads, your encouragement, your writing sessions, your talent, and your friendship. Love you, Poodle.

To my writing community: You know who you are and you know the role you've played in every piece of writing I've completed over the last few years. From the bottom of my heart, thank you. A special thanks to my early readers and my Launch Team and to Stefanie and Kelly for ALL the talks, support, and encouragement.

To Erin: Thank you for giving Birdie a new name.

To my family: Thank you for never, *ever* discouraging my dream. And to my mom; Angela and all the other strong women I write would not exist without your influence. Thank you for being you.

To my dad: Thank you for leaving behind your love of words, art, and beauty. You live on in everything I create.

About the Author

Allison Spooner is the author of two collections of genre-crossing flash fiction, *Flash in the Dark* and *The Problem with Humans*, and has contributed to several horror and science fiction anthologies. This is her debut novel.

Allison is also the founder of Creative Warrior, a program that helps writers and creatives fight for their creativity and find a P.A.T.H. out of writer's block.

When she isn't writing, Allison loves reading, doing yoga, trying not to kill her plants, watching bad disaster movies, and spending time with her family in her home state of Michigan. You can learn more about Allison and her work on her website; www.allisonspoonerwriter.com

If you enjoyed this book, please consider leaving a review on your preferred platform! Reviews are the best way to help Indie Authors (like me!) get noticed and connect with new readers. So, thank you in advance!

For special offers, new releases, exclusive bonus content, and more please consider joining my mailing list by clicking here or scanning below.

Connect With Me?

f   facebook.com/authorallisonspooner

⬡   instagram.com/authorallisonspooner

▶   youtube.com/c/CreativeWarriorClub

♪   tiktok.com/@authorallisonspooner

www.ingramcontent.com/pod-product-compliance
Lightning Source LLC
Chambersburg PA
CBHW011854300726
48970CB00009B/2790